Isabel and the Miracle Baby

Emily Smith Pearce

Front Street
Asheville, North Carolina

For my husband and my parents—EP

Copyright © 2007 by Emily Smith Pearce
Printed in China
Designed by Helen Robinson
First edition

Library of Congress Cataloging-in-Publication Data
Pearce, Emily Smith.
Isabel and the miracle baby / Emily Smith Pearce. — 1st ed.
p. cm.
Summary: Eight-year-old Isabel feels her mother no longer cares about her
because she has no time or energy even to listen when Isa tries to share her
sadness about being unpopular, her jealousy over her new baby sister, and,
most importantly, her fear that her mother's cancer will come back.
ISBN 978-1-932425-44-4 (hardcover : alk. paper)
[1. Mothers and daughters—Fiction. 2. Babies—Fiction.
3. Family life—Fiction. 4. Cancer—Fiction. 5. Friendship—Fiction.
6. Schools—Fiction. 7. Behavior—Fiction.] I. Title.
PZ7.P3412Isa 2007
[Fic]—dc22   2006101750

Front Street
An Imprint of Boyds Mills Press, Inc.
815 Church Street
Honesdale, Pennsylvania 18431

Isabel and the Miracle Baby

Miracle Baby

When Mama was in the kitchen, Isabel grabbed a handful of the baby's wispy brown hair and yanked. It felt good. Good to hear the baby screaming and wailing. Good to see it screwing up its face.

Isabel had asked to go to the park, but Mama said no, the baby was sleeping, and no, they couldn't just leave it behind. "Rebekah needs to nap in her crib, Isabel. You have a baby sister now, and you're going to have to adjust to some things," she said.

Isabel had been adjusting for four months, and she was tired of it.

Miracle baby, the sick ladies called it, because Mama had been sick before she got pregnant. But it screamed like any old baby. Isabel hid under her bed with Clyde the frog and waited for Mama's running footsteps. They went straight to the crib.

Mama bent over and picked up the baby. It stopped

screaming and began to whimper. "What's the matter, honey? Hush now. Mama's here." Her feet in their pink slippers paced back and forth. "Go back to sleep, sweetie. Everything's all right."

She should burn those slippers. Throw them out. When Mama was sick she had worn them every day. Slippers and pajamas and a scarf around her head. She should dress up now. Wear skirts and comb her hair. But with the baby she was still in her robe even in the afternoons, and her hair was rumpled and dirty. She used to have long, dark hair sweeping her shoulders.

The grit under the bed dug into Isabel's sweaty knees. Mama was right there. Isabel could've reached out and grabbed her foot and scared her silly.

Mama patted the baby against her chest. "Isa, where are you?" she said. "Isabel?" She walked out of the room. "I need to talk to you, honey," she called down the hall.

Isabel waited a moment. Mama wasn't coming back. She hadn't even stopped to look under the bed.

It had been Isabel's room until the baby came along. She had to move all her stuffed animals and books under her bed to make space for the baby's crib. Why couldn't Mama and Daddy share *their* room with the baby if they wanted it so much? *They* could have the stinky diaper smell in their faces all the time.

Isabel sneaked to the living room and knelt by the green couch. Her friend Tara should be home by now. If she could just slip through the gap in the chain-link fence, she would be at Tara's house in no time flat. Ms. Pam let them do whatever they wanted, even do experiments in the kitchen, especially when she'd had to work the night shift. There were always lots of kids to play with over there.

Friday Tara had sneaked her mother's cigarettes into the back yard. She and Isabel sat in the corner behind a bush.

"Mama says smoking is bad," Isabel said when Tara offered her one of the cigarettes.

"Isn't she high and mighty," Tara said. "You let her tell you what to do?" She struck a match, lit the cigarette, and waved out the match.

Isabel's heart sped up several paces. It felt like she was getting away with something, even if she wasn't holding a cigarette herself.

"Course, you're only eight. When you get to be nine like me, you don't need to hang on your mama anymore." Tara took a drag and began coughing. She stumped out the cigarette in a patch of dirt. "That must've been a rotten one," she said, but she didn't light another.

Isabel had gone home feeling powerful, like she could break all of Mama's rules, like she could pull the baby's hair if she wanted to. She didn't need to hang on Mama anymore.

While Mama put the baby back to sleep, Isabel inched out of the living room and slipped into the back yard, careful not to bang the aluminum screen door behind her. It was a doughnut day. When the wind blew from the south, it brought the smell of doughnuts from the factory on East Boulevard. An east wind brought steak and onions from Brighton's Restaurant, and sometimes the smell of hot dogs blew in from the soda shop. Everything made her mouth water, but it was doughnut days that made her the hungriest. When Mama was sick and too tired to care, Isabel and Tara used to go to the doughnut factory and buy the messed-up ones for half price.

Isabel crouched by the back stoop and pulled at the clover in the grass. The smell of fabric softener spilled from the dryer vent. Daddy still hadn't put up the swing set like he'd promised. It lay in a heap in the corner of the yard.

Wham! The aluminum door flew open. "Isa!"

Isabel made a mad dash for the fence, but Mama cut her off, grabbing her wrists. "Where are you going?" Mama asked.

Isabel looked down. "Nowhere," she said.

"You're going nowhere pretty fast." Mama marched Isabel to the back steps and made her sit down.

Isabel stared at Mama's yellow toenails.

"Did you bother the baby?" Mama said.

Isabel scowled. "I haven't been near that baby." The baby was *always* crying. At night when it was bedtime, and every time it ate, and when it spit up or filled its diaper.

Mama stared her down for a moment, but Isabel didn't give in. "Never mind about the baby now," Mama said. "Daddy and me decided you can't play with them anymore." She nodded toward Tara's house.

What? Isabel jerked her hands from Mama's and stood up. "You can't tell me what to do!" It was hard to breathe. They couldn't take Tara away too, like they'd taken her room.

Mama grabbed Isabel's elbows and said in a lower voice, "You had cigarette ash on your clothes the other day!" It seemed like she was daring Isabel to deny it.

Isabel just glared.

"Her mother has no idea what you're doing half the time."

Isabel tried to pull away. "She's my friend!" *My only friend*, she thought.

Mama stood up, hands on her hips. "Well, you're going to have to find a new one."

Isabel crossed her arms and planted her feet on the ground. A new friend? Who? The other kids in the neighborhood were either too old or too little, and the kids at school were snobs.

Mama reached out and touched her shoulder, and Isabel stepped back.

"We've got to go to the grocery store when Rebekah wakes up," Mama said.

"No!" Isabel turned and stomped toward the house.

Mama followed her. "I'm not asking, Isa. You're going to go."

Isabel spun to face her, still scowling. "Baby too?"

Mama sighed. "Well, of course the baby. Did you think I would leave Rebekah here?"

"You said we couldn't go to the park because the baby was sleeping."

"We don't have time to go to the park, Isabel. I'm too exhausted anyway."

Isabel turned away again. "Because of the baby," she said, whipping open the screen door and letting it bang against the house. She hoped it would wake the baby up again.

In the car, Isabel kicked the back of Mama's seat over and over again. Mama would change her mind about Tara when she needed to get rid of Isabel. On one of those days when Mama was too tired or too busy with the baby.

At the grocery store the baby rode in the cart while

Isabel had to walk. She grabbed her free cookie from the cookie tray, and when Mama turned to look over the apples and bananas, Isabel ran ahead to the soft-drink aisle. She stood with her back against a display of two-liter Cokes and munched on her cookie. It would take Mama a long time to find her here. She could wait.

The label on the Coke bottle said you could win a video game if you saved enough points. Mama would never let her play video games, but Isabel didn't care what Mama said. She was going to play with Tara anyhow. Mama wouldn't notice. All she noticed was whatever the baby wanted.

A boy with a red vest and a nametag pushed a cart past Isabel and stopped. "Are you okay? Are you lost?" He had a smudge of dark hair on his upper lip.

"I'm fine," she said, pulling at the plastic Coke label. He was going to give her away.

"Where's your mom?" the boy asked.

Isabel narrowed her eyes at him. "I don't have to tell you."

Mama's voice rose above the store music. "Isabel! Isabel Graham, you'd better come out, wherever you are!"

"Are you Isabel?" the boy asked.

"I came to the store by myself," Isabel said. "Leave me alone!"

He left the aisle and then came back, bringing Mama with him. "Is this Isabel?" he asked.

"Yes, thank you," Mama said, and the boy returned to his stock cart.

Mama had her hands on her hips again. "Isa, you had me worried sick. Someone could've taken you." She pulled Isabel tight to her. Mama smelled like baby powder and soap. "You know better than to run off like that. It's not funny. I'm going to tell your daddy."

Isabel pulled her head back. "But, Mama, I was lost!"

Mama looked into Isabel's eyes. "Come on now, Isa. It's hard to get lost if you stay with me. It's easy to get lost if you hide behind Coke bottles. Let's finish the shopping."

She pulled Isabel by the hand and steered the grocery cart back through the store. The miracle baby lay wide-eyed in its carrier, spit dribbling down its chin. Isabel pulled her hand out of Mama's but followed beside the cart. Mama had been worried sick about her. She had missed her right away.

Fire Drill

In the morning Mama stood in the driveway, baby on her hip, while Isabel walked to the bus stop.

"You come straight home after school," Mama called after her.

Where else would I go? Isabel thought, but of course Mama meant *Don't go over to Tara's house.* She'd never been over to anyone else's house because nobody else ever invited her.

Isabel would just have to wait until Mama forgot about Tara. Anyway, Mama couldn't stop her from seeing Tara on the bus.

Tara headed to their favorite seat, right on top of the wheel of the bus. She scooted over to make room for Isabel.

"You coming over this afternoon?" Tara said. Her hair was in a ponytail, clipped back with new purple barrettes. She smelled like Sweet Tarts.

"I can't come over today." Isabel tapped her feet on the wheel hump.

"Why not?"

Isabel picked at the silver tape patching up a hole in the seat. She couldn't tell her what Mama had said.

"Mama says I have to help her with the baby." That sounded boring. "And then I have a dance lesson later." That sounded better. She wished she could twirl around in a pink fluffy skirt, but Mama said there wasn't enough money for that.

Tara sniffed. "Yeah? Well, I have a bunch of other friends coming over anyway."

Isabel smoothed the denim skirt of her dress. "Who?"

"Nobody you would know. Older kids."

Older kids. Older than Tara? Middle schoolers? Isabel would be doing her homework and watching the baby drool while Tara was having a party. At Tara's house they would throw a football in the yard, maybe watch cartoons or a movie.

"Maybe I can sneak out to see you," Isabel said.

"You do whatever your *mama* tells you," Tara said.

Isabel's face burned. She was *not* a baby.

The bus ride was short. They crossed a big city street and passed the park before pulling up to the school. On the sidewalk they lined up according to grade. Tara's line split off to the right, and she was already laughing with the girl next to her.

The school smelled like germs and mildew. Isabel dragged her hand along the yellow cinderblock walls, brushing her fingers across paper lizards the first graders had made and taped up.

The girls in Mrs. Shemeleski's class would be waiting for her, the ones who didn't ride the bus. With their pretty clothes and their matching pink and purple notebooks and cat-shaped erasers. They would be right past the door. Alicia and the other girls were always talking about Isabel. In the hall, in the bathroom, their sentences started with *She ... She ... She.*

Isabel's family had moved here after kindergarten. When she started first grade two years ago, Alicia made fun of her pants and pigtails. All the pink and purple girls wore skirts and low ponytails then.

Their mothers drove them to and from school every day, even though they lived close enough to walk. Their houses were just as old as Isabel's, but they looked new, and they were three times as big, with brick fences and swimming pools peeking out from behind.

She had to sit in front of Courtney, who was new this year. Courtney seemed to have been adopted into Alicia's circle already. Today they were all wearing barrettes with pennies glued to them, and they giggled as Isabel walked past. She put her book bag away and sat down at her desk. There were already ten whole sentences on the board to be copied.

But while she was still correcting the sentences, the alarm bell rang. Fire!

"Put your pencils down," Mrs. Shemeleski said. They stood up row by row and filed out of the classroom.

Isabel left her rainbow pencil sitting on her desk. No one would take it, would they? No one was allowed to stay back. She lined up behind the boy with the squished ears and kept her hands by her sides.

Was it a real fire? Would the school burn down? She should've taken her rainbow pencil with her. It might get burned up sitting there on her desk. But then, Alicia's things might get burned up too. Those pink and purple notebooks. It would be worth losing the rainbow pencil for that.

In the school parking lot, Isabel stood on her toes, trying to find Tara in the fourth-grade crowd. The sun glowed so bright through the pear trees it stung her eyes. She could just see the tip of Tara's ponytail bobbing as she talked to some girl next to her. Isabel lowered her heels, crunching the sand on the asphalt. If the school burned down, they couldn't come back for weeks. Maybe she would have to go with Tara and the fourth graders to a new building.

But after a few minutes the principal blew the whistle, and they all filed back inside. Only a drill. No fire trucks, even. Alicia's things and the rainbow pencil were right where they had been before.

"Put your vocabulary away now," Mrs. Shemeleski said. "We'll finish that later." She talked about why the fire drill was important, and then she announced a field trip to the fire station the next Thursday. "Who has a parent who might be able to come with us?"

For a few seconds no one answered. Isabel could hardly keep her palms flat on the desk. Alicia raised her hand first. Her mother was always at the school. She packed brownies in Alicia's lunches.

"Thank you, Alicia," Mrs. Shemeleski said. Alicia beamed, and then suddenly Isabel's hand was up in the air, too.

Mrs. Shemeleski turned to her. "Isabel," she said. "Very good. I'll call your parents tonight, girls."

Mama would come, right? She had to. It was for school. Her mother was as good and as pretty as Alicia's.

During math Alicia had to do a problem on the board. She sashayed up to the front in her swirly purple skirt, but when she was done, the answer was wrong. A cackle came tumbling out of Isabel's mouth before she could hold it back.

Mrs. Shemeleski pulled her lips together tight and raised her eyebrows at Isabel. Right before lunch she pulled Isabel aside in the hall. The teacher was going to give another one of her "little talks."

Isabel crossed her arms and stood with her feet apart.

Mrs. Shemeleski licked her thin, pale lips. "Laughing at other people's mistakes is not the way to make friends. We've talked about this, Isabel."

Yes, they had. But Mrs. Shemeleski didn't understand. Alicia was mean, but no one ever gave *her* "little talks," and besides, she wasn't trying to make Alicia her friend.

"But she's always saying stuff about me," Isabel said.

The teacher frowned. "I doubt that's true, and at any rate it's no excuse for making fun of her in front of the class." Mrs. Shemeleski's bottom teeth were crowded like a picket fence bunched over on itself. "Would you want someone to laugh at you?"

"I don't care." Isabel scratched her leg with her shoe.

"Well, *I* care," Mrs. Shemeleski said. "I don't want anyone laughing at you, and I don't want you laughing at your classmates. Understood?"

"Yes, ma'am," Isabel said. The red floor tiles lined up row by row all the way out the door.

On the way to lunch, Tara was passing in the other direction through the hall. Isabel waved, but Tara didn't look at her. Isabel turned backward, trying to catch a glimpse of Tara. Why didn't she wave?

"Isabel, face the front of the line," Mrs. Shemeleski said. "Hands to yourself."

Isabel scowled. "All I was doing—"

Mrs. Shemeleski shooed her on through the line. "It doesn't matter, Isabel. Just keep walking."

Of course it didn't matter to *her*. Didn't matter that Isabel's best friend wouldn't wave to her. That her mother wouldn't even let them play together. It didn't matter to Mrs. Shemeleski that none of the other girls liked her.

Mama wouldn't go to the fire station with Isabel's class.

"You should have asked me first. I have a doctor's appointment with Rebekah," she said, sitting on the green corduroy couch. She held the baby in her arms, and it smiled at Isabel as if it thought they were friends.

"But I told them you would go!" Isabel's voice was high and tight. She felt it stretching, stretching, until she thought it might break.

"Well, you'll have to tell them I can't. I can't reschedule this appointment. Really, Isa. You know to ask first before you volunteer me."

Isabel held in the tears so tight her head ached. She flopped down on the soft dusty carpet and dug her fingers into it. Mama got up and laid her free hand on Isabel's shoulder. "Isa," she said. "Come on now—don't be upset. I'll explain to your teacher. She'll understand."

The baby's dried spit-up had made a sour, crusty spot in the rug. Isabel sprang back up. "She will not! She'll give me an F." She had known all along that Mama wouldn't come. "If it weren't for the baby!"

"Isabel, call her Rebekah. Say it. She's your sister."

The miracle baby didn't feel like a sister. It was like some grunting animal that wasn't potty-trained. The baby never had to be patient or quiet or play by itself. Everyone had told her how great it would be to have a brother or sister, how they would play together and look after each other, but the baby couldn't do anything but lie there and take all the attention.

Isabel glared at the baby, who was still smiling. "Rebekah!" Isabel said loudly, right in the baby's face. "There, I said it." She stomped out the back door and sat in the grass by the dryer vent, pulling at the clover.

She had wanted to name the baby Nina, but no one listened to her. The baby didn't look like a Rebekah or a Nina, either. It was floppy and fat-cheeked like a Mildred.

Daddy got home that night and lay on the couch with his long legs draped over the end. He would have a whole day off now, and he could sleep at home tonight because the flooring company was done with the job in Robeson County. Mama warmed up the rest of the beef stew for him.

Isabel stood in front of the television in her ruffled nightgown. "Hey, Daddy," she said, the blue light flickering behind her.

He sat up. "Baby, come here and give your daddy a hug." He pulled her onto his lap. "How are you?"

Isabel rubbed his whiskery cheek. He smelled like sawdust and sweat. She put her hands on either side of his neck. "Mama said I can't play with Tara."

Daddy tucked Isabel's hair behind her ear. "Your mama's afraid you're growing up too fast," he said.

"Daddy, but it's not fair. Tara's my best friend." Isabel leaned her head against his.

He stroked her hair. "Is she really a good friend to you?"

Isabel sat back. "Yes, Daddy! You got to tell Mama."

Daddy rested his heavy, broad hand on top of her head. "Your mama said you come back from Tara's talking back and smelling like smoke. What's my little girl doing with cigarette ash on her clothes?"

Isabel pulled away and stood up. "Mama's lying! She just doesn't want me to have any friends."

Daddy took Isabel's shoulders in his hands. "You don't talk about your mama like that, you hear?"

"I don't have anybody else but Tara." Didn't he know that?

"My pretty girl, don't you have lots of friends at school?"

"No." She crossed her arms and looked away. If he made her say anything else she wouldn't be able to hold in the tears.

"I love you, honey," Daddy said.

Isabel pulled at her nightgown and took a deep breath. "Can you go on the field trip with us next Thursday? We're going to the fire station. Mama won't come."

Daddy rubbed his whiskers. "I have to work," he said.

Isabel bounced up and down on her feet. "You could take the day off."

He swept her hair back from her forehead. "Honey, you know I got to work when there's work. I'm sorry. I wish I could go." Daddy pulled her to him and kissed her on the cheek.

She squirmed away.

Mama walked in. "It's time for bed, Isa," she said.

"I can put myself to bed," Isabel said. She was hoping Daddy would offer to tell her stories about Clyde the frog, but he didn't. He was always too tired now, if he was even home.

Under her yellow-rose bedspread Isabel balled herself into a knot. Back at their old house near the ocean, Daddy had his own fix-it shop and came home every night to put her to bed. There was no baby, and Mama was never sick. Isabel had friends at school. If Daddy hadn't closed the shop they would still be there, and everything would be better.

The Sick Ladies

Daddy left for another out-of-town job, and the sick ladies met at their house again on Tuesday. Isabel had to sit in the circle with them, even though she wasn't a sick lady. Mama wasn't sick anymore either, and she wasn't going to be sick again, like some of those ladies. Not if Isabel had anything to do with it. She was through with cancer.

The dining room chairs were arranged in a semicircle near the corduroy couch.

Isabel's job was to hand out plastic cups of iced tea and the lemon cookies Mama had bought at the store. Meanwhile Tara was probably at the park playing with older kids. "You have fun with your *mama*," she had said on the bus ride home.

Isabel held out a plastic cup to the puffy-cheeked lady in the green jumpsuit. "You want some tea?" she said. That lady was always wearing that jumpsuit. Isabel slopped some tea on the woman's hand. "Sorry," Isabel said.

The woman waved her hand like it was no big deal. "That's all right, honey," she said. "I'm waterproof."

"Could I have some tea, please, ma'am?" the stirrup-pants lady next to her asked.

Isabel kept her eyes down and went from one lady to the next, handing out cups. The ladies gave each other recipes for low-fat brownies and complained about their daughters' boyfriends.

The sick ones looked the way Mama had, with dry lips covered in sores and skin smelling like forks from the cafeteria. Some wore lots of makeup, some none at all, leaving their faces gray, wearing their sores right out in the open. Didn't they know how *awful* they looked?

If Mama didn't want cancer again, maybe she shouldn't hang out with these ladies. Isabel was always hearing that you couldn't catch it like that, but she wasn't so sure. You couldn't trust cancer.

Maybe Mama would dress up more if she hung around other people. These ladies didn't know how to dress. They wore sweatpants and too-big shirts and worn-out shoes. Most of them had short-short hair like a man's. Or worse, none at all.

Not all of the ladies were sick. Some of them were well now, like Mama. And Mrs. Andos, who was walking in now, filling up the room with her big shoulders. She had loose, dark curls and a sharp nose that meant business. She was one of the good ones. It was hard to believe she had ever had cancer.

"Is Janey coming?" Isabel asked her. Janey Andos was fourteen. Sometimes she did Isabel's hair during the kids' playtime. When the baby was born, Isabel had stayed with the Andoses, and they fed her ice cream and took her to the movies and the aquarium. She wished Janey were her sister instead of the little blob.

Mrs. Andos sighed. "Janey has volleyball practice on Tuesdays now," she said. "The season started last week."

"Oh," Isabel said, holding on tight to another cup of tea. Janey had been the only good thing about these meetings.

"How's school?" Mrs. Andos asked.

Isabel handed her the cup of tea. "We're going on a field trip to the fire station. Mama was supposed to come with us, but she won't go."

Mama turned to them. "Isa," she said, warning her.

Well, it was true, wasn't it?

A new lady walked in with a boy of at least seven or eight who was sucking his thumb. Didn't he know he was too old for that? The lady wore a pink scarf knotted around her head, which probably meant she was bald, and the boy hid behind her. He was very small, a shrimp, with a big, pale forehead. Isabel could see it already: they'd make her play with him. He was probably a wimp and a crybaby. Isabel gave the new lady a cup of iced tea, and the woman sat down with her son in the chairs that were backed up to the TV.

Isabel picked up the plate of lemon cookies.

The green-jumpsuit lady was grabbing Stirrup Pants by the arm. "You know what you should do?" she was saying. "Just shave it off, honey. I promise you'll feel better. You look like a kewpie doll."

Stirrup Pants had only a tufted stripe of hair down the middle of her head. Mama had been bald just like that. Isabel got the shivers when she thought about it. "Well, thank you," said Stirrup Pants, sounding as if she didn't much want the advice.

"You'll feel like a new person."

"A *bald* person."

"I hate to tell you, honey, but you're already bald, in case you hadn't noticed!"

Why wouldn't Mama grow out her hair again? She didn't have cancer anymore. It seemed like she was just waiting for cancer to come back. Did she think if her hair was short then it wouldn't matter if it fell out again?

Isabel shivered at the thought, nearly dropping the cookies.

The ladies looked at Isabel as if they'd forgotten she

was standing there. Stirrup Pants gave her a fake, sugary smile. "I bet you're a big help to your mama with the new baby. You're such a big girl now."

Isabel held out the plate of cookies, and the ladies took some.

"I'm not so big," Isabel said. The sick ladies were the ones who called it a miracle baby. When Mama's belly was huge, they had a party for the baby. After all of that strong medicine from the chemo it had to be a miracle, they said. They gave Isabel bows from the presents like she was supposed to be happy she got anything. What was she supposed to do with a bunch of bows?

Mrs. Andos was holding the baby up. She kissed its cheek. "She's so sweet." She turned to Isabel. "Isn't she sweet, Isabel? You must love your little sister so much."

Isabel pressed her lips together. Mrs. Andos didn't seem so great right now.

"That's a real pretty dress you have on, Isa," Stirrup Pants said.

Isabel turned away and went back to passing out cookies. They thought they could call her Isa just because they knew Mama.

Everyone began to sit down and get quiet.

Mama called to her. "You can stop passing cookies. It's time to sit down now."

"I've got to put them away," Isabel said, edging toward the kitchen. Maybe she could just sneak out the back, and they'd forget about her. She'd find Tara and her older friends at the park.

"Come on, Isa. Just set them down and sit with us," Mama said.

"They'll go stale."

"Come."

Isabel huffed and put the cookie tray down, taking a seat on the floor beside Mama. She could have a chair if she wanted, but the floor was better. She didn't have to look at the big-haired lady's painted-on face. If Isabel kept her head cocked just this way and didn't move, maybe no one would see her.

"Let's get started," Big Hair said.

People quieted down.

"All right, folks, we have some new faces with us this afternoon." Big Hair motioned to the woman with the boy. "This is Linda and her son, Benjamin. Linda, why don't you tell us a little bit about yourself?"

Linda looked around the room. "We moved here from Asheville ten years ago," she said. She was wearing ripped jeans and a toe ring. "I'm a florist. We found out I was sick a few months ago." She looked at the boy. "You want to introduce yourself, honey?"

The boy gulped.

She put her hand on his shoulder. "This is Ben," she said. "He likes to play on the computer, don't you, sweetie?" She smiled and hugged him to her.

Play on the computer? No wonder he looked like a pale shrimp. Playing computer didn't make you big and strong. Or popular. He must play on computers because he didn't have any friends. Or maybe it was the other way around—he didn't have any friends because all he did was play on the computer. He moved closer to his mom like he was afraid somebody might attack him.

"Thank you, Linda. We're glad to have you with us." The big-haired lady made some announcements, and then they moved on to the question of the day. Today's question was, *If you could have a day to do anything you wanted, what would you do?*

Well, that was easy. Isabel would go over to Tara's for the whole day. They'd walk over to the park and then get doughnuts at the doughnut factory. Then back at Tara's they'd watch cartoons, and Tara would braid her hair. Not that Isabel was going to tell Big Hair this.

The ladies said things like they'd run a marathon or they'd eat whatever they felt like. Or sleep until they weren't tired anymore, with good dreams.

"I know what you mean," one woman said. "I'm so tired

I can't stay awake. I just want to dig down and hibernate."

"Pass," Isabel said when it was her turn. "You can say 'pass' if you don't want to talk."

Some of the ladies chuckled. Had she said something funny?

The boy's mother said she just wanted to be nice for a whole day.

Nice?

"I yell at my family," she said. "I have no patience."

What a dumb thing to ask for. When you could do anything. *Nice.*

Her little boy looked like he'd just woken up. He was downright ugly and skinny with ears that stuck out like doorknobs and hair smashed down on one side. Would he answer the question? He'd probably want to play on the computer all day. He whispered something into his mother's ear.

"Ben thinks he'll pass this time," she said.

Scaredy-cat.

The women kept on jabbering while Isabel dug her fingers into the soft brown carpet. She could hear laughter coming from Tara's back yard.

Finally she could go.

"You and Ben can go play outside for a while. Be nice," Mama said, with a hard look.

Isabel shot her the evil eye. The boy was a little shrimp, and there weren't any computers outside.

Shrimp Boy hid behind his mother, who leaned over and whispered something in his ear, smiling at him. Probably telling him Isabel wouldn't bite. Well, she would if she needed to. She had to protect herself.

Outside, Isabel ran ahead through the thick grass and let him follow. When she got to the fence, Tara and whoever else was next door had gone inside. What were they doing without her? Not talking with sick ladies or shrimp boys, that was for sure.

"You want to climb the tree or something?" Isabel asked, grabbing onto a low-hanging branch of the big oak tree.

"No," he said, picking at a huge azalea bush by the chain-link fence.

"Are you scared?" She swung back and forth. Isabel wasn't allowed to climb the tree, but Mama wasn't paying any attention.

"No!" He jammed his hands in his pockets.

"Shoot, boy, what are you afraid of? It's only a little tree. You won't fall out unless you do something stupid." She hooked her feet around the branch.

"My mom said—"

"Listen to you—'My mom said.' Aren't you a little mama's boy!"

His eyes turned mean. "No!" He started stomping back to the house.

Isabel dropped to the ground and ran after him, grabbing him around the waist and nearly toppling him.

"Running to your mama now?" she said. No way was this little runt getting her in trouble.

He was stronger than he looked. He kept moving toward the house, dragging her while she clung to his waist. Suddenly he stopped. They could hear voices inside.

Isabel clambered up the concrete steps to the back door.

"What do you mean by 'sensitive'?" Big Hair was asking.

Mama's voice. "She gets upset over little things," she said. "She doesn't like the baby. Sometimes I don't know what to do with her."

Mama was saying things about her, bad things. It was none of the ladies' business!

Isabel threw open the door and stormed into the room. She didn't bother trying to keep her voice down. "You were laughing at me!"

The baby looked out at her from Mama's arms, listening to everything.

Mama lowered her eyes. "No, honey. That's not it." She reached out a hand, but Isabel pulled back. "Isabel,"

Mama said. "Isabel." She took Isabel by the arm this time, and held tight.

Isabel yanked away, her face breaking out in a sweat. All the ladies were staring at her. Even the baby with its dark eyes, staring at her.

"Isabel," Mama said, very calm, level, so just Isabel could hear. "Why don't you go back outside with Ben?"

"I'm not playing with him any more!"

"Isabel," Mama said, harder this time.

Mama's calm voice could make her explode. *"No!"* Isabel said.

"Excuse us," Mama said, and she was mad now. Finally, she was mad. "You go on, Brenda," she said, and handed the baby to the woman next to her. The ladies smiled the aren't-we-glad-we-aren't-your-mother smile, and Mama yanked Isabel into the hall.

"Go to your room now. You wait there until you've calmed down."

"I don't have to go anywhere! You can't tell me what to do! I hate you!"

Mama pushed Isabel into her room by the small of her back. "We'll talk later," she said, in a voice that meant, *You're going to get it.* Then she walked out and pulled the door shut behind her.

Isabel banged on the door. "You can't lock me up in

here," she shouted. "I'm going to call the police on you!" But she knew it wasn't really locked.

So *that* was what they did when the kids left to play—said nasty things about her. She was never falling for that trick again. They probably went home and told everyone what a rotten kid she was. She braced herself against the wall, waiting for the voices to die down and the ladies to file out. They were never going to leave, and now she was stuck in this room that wasn't her room anymore that smelled like dirty diapers. She pulled one end of the crib away from the wall. She would wheel it into Mama and Daddy's room.

But Mama marched into Isabel's room without knocking. "Isabel, you can't disrupt the meeting like that."

"You were talking about me!"

Mama looked at the crib and, without saying anything, moved it back into place. "You don't even know what we were talking about," she said. "You embarrassed me."

Embarrassed her! Embarrassed *her!* Isabel sputtered. *She* was the one who was embarrassed. "You! ... You!"

That was all she could get out. If she said another word the tears would spill out all over the place. She wanted to hit Mama, throw things at her. She picked up Clyde the frog and threw him hard against the wall.

Mama grabbed her wrists hard. "You just calm down, Isabel. That is no way to act." Again, her voice was level, in control, and it only made Isabel crazier.

Then Mama left, like it was no big deal. She didn't even say she was sorry. She didn't take anything back.

Isabel squeezed into a tight ball on her yellow-rose bedspread. *Embarrassed her!* It was too much. She curled into a quiet pocket so everything would stay where it should. She could breathe in and out, in and out, and a calm space would open up inside. In, out; in, out. The tears dried up before they ever came. She lay quiet now, let her head and chest rest, breathing slow and safe.

Mama and Daddy had never asked her if she wanted a miracle baby. They hadn't even told her about the baby at first, and she'd thought Mama must be sick again, the way she threw up all the time. When they finally showed her a picture of the baby inside Mama, it didn't look like a baby at all—just some alien ghost.

Little things. Little? They were little only to Mama. Was having no friends a little thing? Was sharing her room a little thing?

Sensitive. She held the word to her, not letting it spill out. If she threw it against the wall it would bounce back, hard, and hit her in the stomach. She breathed it out until it was just a word. *Sensitive.* It didn't mean anything at all.

It didn't matter what those ladies knew about her. Who cared who they were?

The yellow curtains lifted in the breeze, and Isabel breathed in and out until she fell asleep, her eyelet socks still on and homework left undone.

The Blackout

But in the morning the word was smack dab in front of her. *Sensitive.* The baby woke up crying before dawn.

"The *baby* is sensitive!" Isabel said, and she stored the word away.

"She's just hungry. Go back to sleep, Isa," Mama said, smoothing her hair.

Isabel wiped away the feel of Mama's hand on her head. She couldn't fall back to sleep. Mama still hadn't apologized for yesterday.

That morning at school Mrs. Shemeleski drew a house on the board the way it would look from an airplane if it didn't have a roof. Then she made arrows. It was a fire-escape plan. She said you could even keep a rope ladder in your room if your house was high off the ground or had two stories. A rope ladder! Isabel wished they had two stories. Maybe she would make a rope ladder anyway. She'd keep it hidden under her bed and sneak out whenever she needed to escape.

There was one bit of good news: the fourth grade, including Tara's class, would be coming on the field trip too. Mama couldn't keep them apart there.

But Tara didn't even ask her over anymore when they rode home on the bus. She hopped off the bus and ran into her house without looking back.

Mama was standing in the yard, holding the baby, making sure Isabel came straight home, no playing with Tara.

"You cut your hair!" Isabel said. It didn't even cover her ears now.

Mama tried to fluff it up, but it barely moved. "I know. It's short, isn't it? It's easy. I don't have to do anything to it."

Isabel scowled and walked past her into the house. Mama didn't have to have short hair anymore. Why couldn't she let it grow? You were *supposed* to have to do things with your hair.

For homework she had to draw an escape plan from her house. This was hard. How did the rooms look from the sky? Isabel and the baby's room was next to Mama and Daddy's, and the living room was in front and the kitchen in back, but when she drew it they looked all wrong. She had made the kitchen the size of the bathroom, and the house wasn't square.

Isabel drew her room in purple, the color she had always wanted it to be, with the baby a tiny spot in it. Better yet, she put the baby in the closet. What did it need windows for? She drew escape arrows to the back yard—no, the front yard was where you were supposed to go in case of a fire.

You might have to have lots of plans of escape so you could be ready no matter what. You were supposed to have a family meeting to talk about where you would go if a fire started in your home. Daddy was away in Fayette County, laying down floors. Mama was in the den nursing the baby. Maybe she wouldn't even tell them. Mama would be sorry when a fire came and she didn't know what to do.

Isabel would go in the living room, just to look, just to see what Mama would say. Maybe Isabel would tell Mama about the escape plan if she would listen. If she would pay any attention. But Mama looked up from the baby and smiled, as if to say, *Isn't she cute?* Isabel turned around and left.

She might as well be at the after-school program for all the help Mama gave her. At least she got to see Tara there. Isabel had gone to the after-school in first grade when Mama was too sick to sit up. Dragon Lady with her scaly skin and her flaring nostrils told her to hush, it was quiet time, and if Isabel whispered just a little bit Dragon Lady took her snack, and then Isabel didn't have anything to eat until suppertime.

"You come here every day?" Tara had said the first time they met. She was skinny and muscle-y and wearing a yellow tank top with daisies.

Isabel looked up from copying words onto lined paper.

"I only come when I feel like it," Tara said. "Don't you live next door? I've seen you before out in the yard."

Isabel's family had lived there since the summer, and Isabel had seen her in the yard, too. There were always lots of kids at that house, and she had been too shy to introduce herself.

Tara sat down and leaned toward Isabel like they were good friends. "Don't take nothing off those ladies. They can shush all they want, but they can't make you do anything."

Tara had made the place bearable. She made school bearable, but Mama didn't understand.

Tara was probably just behind the fence now, playing with somebody else. If the baby hadn't screamed bloody murder just because she pulled its hair a little bit, Isabel would be over there, too. *Sensitive!*

Isabel traced over the lines of her house plan.

Mama called from the kitchen. "Isa! It's time to eat. Wash your hands."

Isabel sat there not washing her hands. She waited until Mama called her again, then walked to the kitchen. Chicken bog for supper. Isabel wrinkled her nose.

"I thought you liked chicken bog," Mama said. The baby sat propped on Mama's lap while she ate.

Isabel did like chicken bog, but she wasn't going to admit it. She picked at the chicken and rice. The baby's eyes stared at nothing as it dribbled spit down its no-neck double chin. "Gross!"

"You haven't eaten anything," Mama said.

"I'm not hungry," Isabel said, but it wasn't true. She could count on Mama to insist that she eat her dinner.

"You won't get anything else to eat."

"Some people have homework to do," Isabel said, getting up from the table and leaving her plate right there.

"Isabel! Sit back down," Mama said. "You have to eat."

Isabel waited in the doorway.

Mama sighed. "You won't get anything else until you've eaten dinner," she said. Isabel stepped slowly into the hallway. But Mama didn't get up.

She was just going to let her go? Mama had never let her get away with that before. Isabel *was* hungry, but going back would be giving in. Isabel walked to her room and closed the door. Before cancer and the baby Mama would never have given up so easily. She would have taken the time to find out what was wrong and to convince her to eat. Isabel went back to her homework. After a while she heard Mama in the bathroom singing to the baby while she bathed it.

There is a ship, and it sails the sea.

She used to sing that song to Isabel. A long, long time ago. Before she even got sick, before her beautiful long hair fell out. She was never going to grow it out again, was she?

Isabel tiptoed by while Mama rubbed sweet-smelling lotion on the baby's stomach and arms. Well, that was a waste. It would be stinky again in no time.

The baby would be going to bed now. Isabel carried her map to the kitchen before Mama could ask her to leave her own room so the baby could sleep.

Isabel pulled the chicken bog out of the fridge. She wanted to heat it up in the microwave, but the noise would let Mama know she had given in, so she ate it cold, standing up.

Later Mama leaned on the kitchen doorframe and smiled. Her smile said, *Here I am*—as if Isabel would be happy about that. So she was here, now that the *baby* was fed and asleep, now that the *baby* had what it wanted. Mama didn't even care if Isabel ate her supper.

"I see you got something to eat," she said, looking at the dishes.

Isabel wished she had put the dishes away already. Now Mama thought she had won: she had gotten Isabel to eat without even trying.

"Do you need help with your spelling words?" Mama asked.

Spelling words! Spelling tests were on Friday. It was only Wednesday night. Mama didn't keep up.

"No," Isabel said, keeping her eyes down as she drew on her map. She didn't need any help, and she certainly wasn't going to take it from someone who talked behind her back. She covered the escape plan with her hand.

"What's bothering you?" Mama said.

Isabel set her pencil down and glared at her. If Mama didn't know already, Isabel wasn't going to tell her. Had she already forgotten about yesterday, how she had said bad things about her at the meeting?

Mama hung by the door, waiting. Like she wanted to stay, wanted Isabel to need help.

If she really wanted to help, she would figure out what was the matter, but she didn't. Isabel kept drawing, and Mama left, turned on the music in the den, probably picked up her knitting. She was making a big pink blanket for the baby.

It was raining and raining and raining. The back yard would be filling up with lakes, the way it always did when there was a storm, and the grass would sway like seaweed underwater. Lightning flickered in the distance. Isabel tapped her pencil on the windowsill.

Boom! Thunder crashed and the lights went out. A thrill shot inside Isabel's chest, and she let out a squeal in the dark.

Mama's silhouette appeared at the door. "It's okay, honey. It's just the lights. I'll get some candles."

Isabel huddled until her eyes adjusted. She felt along the walls toward the cabinets even though she could see the way now. Maybe it would stay dark for a long, long time. They might be without electricity for days. At school, too. School would be canceled, and they would have to live like pioneers. Mama would sew Isabel's clothes, and they would wash everything by hand. They'd churn butter from the milk of their backyard cow and gather eggs from their chickens. Their only light would be the sun or candles, and at night they would sit around the fireplace, making s'mores. Daddy would have to stay nearby and find a job where he could walk to work.

Mama stood in her nightgown and slippers, shuffling through the drawers. When she found the candles, she struck a match, and the flame sprang from it like a bright flag.

The candle crackled and spit, wax dripping down the side like icicles. Isabel cupped her hands around it, nearly roasting her palms. It was as if she'd captured some tiny living thing.

She had to be careful, though. What if she knocked it off the counter? The wick might catch on the curtain. The wax would puddle, and the fire would race up the walls.

The flame danced and skittered, as if it was dying to escape this little corner of air.

Fire could be dangerous. People could get burned. *Stop, drop, and roll if the fire gets you. Some people want to run, but this is the wrong thing to do.*

Isabel's hands shook. Fire was a wild thing, an animal you had to keep on a leash. You couldn't turn your back on it.

"Be careful, Isa," Mama said, taking Isabel's hand. Mama's hand on hers felt like an apology, and Isabel forgot what she had been mad about. They were pioneers together, just the two of them.

Gently, Mama took the candle from Isabel and placed it in a glass holder on the counter. Glowing in the candlelight, the kitchen looked warm and cozy, and the green flowered wallpaper didn't look so old. Isabel and Mama watched the candle flame bob and weave. In pioneer days, now would be the time to sit around the fire and tell stories while brushing out each other's hair.

Suddenly the lights buzzed back on, and the candle flame was weak, useless now. Mama blew it out.

The pioneer life vanished, and Isabel blinked in the glare of the ordinary kitchen lights. Mama had already turned to the sink to wash the dishes.

"I'm going to bed now," Isabel said, folding up her map and tiptoeing toward her room where the baby lay asleep.

"Honey," Mama called out after her. "Come kiss me good night."

Isabel kept going.

"All right then. I'll come kiss you later," Mama said.

If Mama did come, it must've been much later, when Isabel was already asleep.

The Fire Station

On the field trip Isabel had to be in Alicia's group, not Tara's. She even had to ride the bus with Alicia's group. How was she ever going to get a chance to win Tara back?

Alicia got to have all *her* friends in the group, and her mother sat right behind them, waves of perfume rolling off her fancy silky sweater topped with pearls.

The floor of the fire station was cool gray concrete. Isabel sat cramped and crowded between her group and the next. She could hit Johnny for brushing her with his elbow, and fat old Mary Ann deserved a pinch on her chubby arm. Isabel sat on her hands. Did they really have to stay here all day?

Mama was supposed to be here, but she was at the doctor with the drippy baby. The baby always got Mama.

"You in the yellow shirt—would you like to hose down a fire?"

Isabel snapped to attention. The dark-haired fireman

was talking to *her*. He had picked *her*. She stood up and walked to the front.

"Let's give her the proper gear first, ladies and gentlemen. First she needs a coat." On it went. "A hat." Down over her head. "Gloves." They were huge.

All eyes were on her, everyone wishing they were Isabel right now. She giggled. The gear was so heavy she could barely stay standing.

"What a smile we have there, folks," the fireman said, smiling back at her. "And now, finally, she needs a hose."

He helped her lift the hose, which was also very heavy, and he pretended they were hosing off a fire high up to one side. "The force of a waterfall would be pumping through there, and that would make it even harder to lift. If you were standing in front of that stream, do you know what would it feel like?"

Someone yelled out, "Like a Slip 'n' Slide?"

"Well, not exactly. It'd just about take your skin off, it's so strong. It has to be if it's going to put out fires." He put the hose down.

"Okay," he said, "but what if a fire starts in your house? What should you do?" He lit a piece of newspaper and dropped it in a small metal trashcan.

Isabel's eyes popped at the way the flame dissolved the paper and turned it into living colors.

"Call 9-1-1?" somebody yelled out.

"That's the second thing you should do. What's the first thing?" He didn't wait for an answer. "Get out of the house! Then call 9-1-1 from a safe location."

Isabel imagined her house in the twisting flames. Mama yelling, baby screaming, Daddy away at work somewhere. She was the only one who could save them.

The fireman held Isabel's hand over the trigger of a fire extinguisher, directing the nozzle toward the fire. White foam shot out, smothering the fire.

The fireman lifted the hat and jacket off her, and she sat down. She was plain old Isabel now, not the firefighting superhero, but she couldn't stop smiling.

Mrs. Shemeleski said it was time for lunch, and everyone had to eat with their group. Isabel could see Tara pulling out her silver-wrapped Pop-Tart over by the fire truck. She didn't look lonely at all.

Isabel sat on the spiky grass outside with Alicia and the others. She pulled out her soggy peanut butter and jelly sandwich. The ground was hard and lumpy.

Alicia and Courtney and Mandy all had Sub Station sandwiches with chips and pickles, and Alicia was passing out Rice Krispies Treats. Mama never made goodies like that or even bought them.

Alicia came over with a treat for Isabel. Her mother

probably made her do it. "Hey, wasn't your mom going to come?" Alicia said.

Isabel looked up. Alicia had better not talk about Mama. She grabbed the Rice Krispies Treat, wanting to throw it at Alicia, but it was too good to pass up. "She had to take the baby to the doctor," Isabel said. That was what Mama had said, right? Or was it go to the doctor with the baby? The baby doctor or the cancer doctor?

Alicia squinched up her nose like she smelled a diaper. "You have a baby brother?"

Isabel picked off a sticky Rice Krispie and mashed it in the dirt. "Sister." Would they be home by now? Was everything okay? She squeezed the treat, and it stuck to her hand. Why didn't Mama take *her* to the cancer doctor?

"I would hate that." Alicia sat down on a piece of paper to keep her pink jeans from getting dirty.

Isabel narrowed her eyes at Alicia. "I do hate it."

Alicia laughed, but it wasn't a mean laugh. "You're funny," she said. It sounded like she meant good funny, not weird funny.

Isabel ate the rest of the Rice Krispies Treat a tiny bite at a time, breathing out through her mouth. Which doctor had Mama gone to? Isabel tried hard to remember exactly what Mama had said, but she couldn't. She threw her peanut butter sandwich in the trash.

Afterward they got a tour of the firehouse and a chance to climb on the fire truck. Isabel raced to the steering wheel. She would drive this big old shiny red truck and be the fire chief, and everyone would have to listen to her. Other kids were clamoring for her seat, but she wouldn't give it up until Mrs. S. gave her one of those warning looks.

Tara was checking out the back of the truck with some other fourth graders. Did she even know Isabel was here?

"Hey, Tara," she called, as she climbed down from the truck.

Tara gave her the tiniest of nods, more of a chin lift. "Hey," she mouthed.

That was okay. Isabel could work with a "hey," even a lousy one.

On the way back to school, Tara sat in the back with some fourth grader who had braids. Isabel had to sit with Courtney on the bus. Courtney sat behind her in class, but they had never talked.

"I hate my little sister, too," Courtney said. "Most of the time." She had on a pink flowered shirt from the Limited.

Isabel fingered her own yellow shirt, which wasn't nearly as pretty. "How old is she?"

"Four." Courtney tapped her shoes together.

"Mine's only a baby."

"They're even worse when they get older," Courtney said. "Trust me."

Isabel smiled.

When they got back to the school parking lot, the regular buses had already come and gone, so everyone's parents had to come pick them up. Little brothers and sisters were crawling around in back seats, and moms were waving from their open car doors. It was back to ordinary everything. Except that Mama wasn't there. She must still be at the doctor's, or did the doctor send her to the hospital? Maybe her hair was already falling out, her face gray like ashes.

Courtney went off with Alicia and Mandy, and they all got picked up right away. Their mothers probably had more Rice Krispies Treats waiting for them.

But Alicia had said she was funny. Good funny. Was she really? No one had ever told her that before.

Isabel squinted at the line of cars sparkling in the afternoon sun. Would Daddy come pick her up instead? She scanned the parking lot for his green truck, but it wasn't there either. How was she going to get home? The other kids were all matching up to cars, and soon she would be the only one left.

Daddy was still out of town, she remembered. Would there be anybody to stay with her tonight? Isabel gulped in air as fast as she could. Was Mama sick again? Would Isabel have to spend the night at school? Walk home? She didn't even have a key. Maybe Mrs. S. would let her stay at her house.

Once when Isabel still went to the after-school program, Mama hadn't showed up at the end of the day. Isabel had waited and waited, doing her words, counting to one hundred, until all the other kids were gone. Finally the Dragon Lady had to call Daddy. Mama had been caught up at the doctor's office and forgotten about her.

All of a sudden there Tara was in front of her. Isabel must've had a funny look on her face because Tara said, "What's the matter? Lost your mama?"

Isabel blinked.

"You want to come home with me?" Tara nodded toward her mother, who was leaning out of their big blue car.

She would get a ride with Tara, and she'd be okay. Tara was still her friend.

"Okay, sure. Yeah." Isabel grabbed her book bag and followed after Tara, wanting to hug her knees for saving her. Mama was sick, but Isabel couldn't think about her right now. Maybe Isabel and Tara would go to the doughnut factory. Maybe Tara would braid her hair or they'd play football with the older kids. She couldn't help it. A big, stupid grin spread across her face. She and Tara slid across the back seat and let their legs dangle.

"Well, hello, Miss Isabel," Ms. Pam said. "Haven't seen you in a while."

"Hey," Isabel said. She wouldn't tell Ms. Pam what Mama had said. *Her mother has no idea what you're doing half the time.*

Tara turned toward her and smiled, an easy smile, and it must mean she was Isabel's friend again.

Mama's car wasn't in the driveway when they got to their street. Isabel wasn't going to think about the cancer doctor. There was nothing she could do about it right now. Isabel followed Tara into her house.

Ms. Pam's soap opera had already started, so they all sat down with handfuls of Cap'n Crunch. Mama wouldn't let her watch soaps at all. Ms. Pam lit her cigarette and blew smoke rings for them.

Isabel lay back on the scratchy plaid couch. In the cool, dark room lit only by the television, she was safe. Nobody fussed at her to be quiet, and she didn't need to say anything anyway.

When the soap opera was over, Isabel and Tara made up a secret code so they could write notes no one else would understand. It was like old times. They were spies sending messages back and forth across enemy territory.

A little later Denise, Tara's cousin, came home from high school with her friend Erica.

"Hey, Denise," Isabel said. Denise was tall and beautiful and stylish.

"Haven't seen you in a while," Denise said, resting her hand on Isabel's head. "Hey, let's do your hair."

Isabel and Tara squealed.

Erica didn't really like younger kids, but she always copied whatever Denise did.

Luckily Isabel got Denise while Tara had Erica pulling at her hair with a hot curling iron. Erica kept holding the curler too long, and a burnt-hair smell filled the room.

Tara screeched. "Erica! What are you doing?"

Denise combed out Isabel's hair and twisted it into little rolls on the back of her head. It had been a long time since anyone had done her hair. Mama said she was a big girl now and could do it herself. Isabel breathed in and blew out. She was not going to think about Mama right now.

Someone rapped at the front door, and Isabel snapped to attention. Nobody ever knocked here. They just walked in the back. It had to be Mama! Sure enough, there was her voice.

"Hi, Pam," Mama said. She sounded angry. "Have you seen Isabel anywhere? She's missing."

Missing? Mama was the one who had been missing. What had happened at the doctor's?

Grinning, Tara turned to Isabel. "Ooh, you're in trouble now."

Denise patted Isabel on the back. "You better go."

She didn't want to go. Her hands broke out in a sweat, and she felt her heart beating in her stomach.

"We picked her up after the field trip since you weren't there," Ms. Pam said.

"I *was* there! I was just a few minutes late!"

She was? Isabel hid behind the door, and Tara burst out laughing.

"Well, it's no big deal," Ms. Pam was saying. "I was happy to take her."

"No big deal? I've been looking for her for three hours! I've had the police out. How dare you? Why didn't you call?"

The police? Mama had called the police? Isabel was going to get it bad. Real bad.

"Now look here, Marsha." Ms. Pam's voice got louder. "You don't come into my house like Miss Do-Right and tell me off when I was trying to help you out."

"Where's Isabel?"

"The girls' room. Remind me never to do you a favor again."

"I didn't ask for a favor." Mama stomped through the house. "Isa!"

Tara turned to Isabel again. "Your mama's got some nerve, coming over here like that."

Isabel scowled. Mama didn't have to make a scene. Now she wouldn't have to keep Isabel from Tara's house. Ms. Pam would see her coming and send her away.

The door creaked open, and Mama popped her head into the room. Her hair was all there. Still short, but she didn't look any different. The baby gave its dumb look like always.

"Bye, Tara," Isabel said, trying to say she was sorry with her eyes. "Bye, Denise. Bye, Erica."

Mama grabbed Isabel's hand with her free one and marched her out the front door past the older boys playing football in the yard. All the kids looked at her like she was a baby. Tara would never play with her ever again.

Back in their yard, Isabel yanked her hand away. Mama spun around and pulled her close. "I have half a mind to spank you," she said.

Mama should be the one getting punished. "You weren't there!"

"I was ten minutes late, Isabel. You can't go off just because I'm not there that minute."

"Where were you?"

"I told you, I was at the doctor's. Isabel, don't you ever go home with them again." She nodded toward Tara's house. "Or anybody. You understand? From now on I'll pick you up after school. Every day."

Isabel searched Mama's face to see if she meant it. She couldn't remember Mama ever picking her up at school. Only the pink and purple mothers did that, and the only reason Mama was doing it now was to keep her from Tara. Had Mama's face changed? Her skin and lips looked normal, not gray and sick. But that didn't mean she couldn't be sick.

Isabel's voice rose to cracking. "Do you have ... are you sick again?" She shifted from one foot to the other.

"Sick?" Mama's face softened. She switched the baby to her other hip. "What makes you think that?"

"You were at the doctor's!" Isabel knew what that meant. Did Mama think she didn't?

Mama put a hand on Isabel's shoulder, holding her still. "I took Rebekah to her doctor, just like I told you."

Isabel stared at a heap of brown leaves, talking very low. "Sometimes the ladies get sick again. I know."

"Sometimes they do, you're right, but I didn't even go to see the cancer doctor," Mama said. She ran her hand over Isabel's hairdo.

"Don't mess it up!" Isabel said, ducking away from her. Her knees felt wobbly.

"I'm healthy, honey," Mama said. "They got all the

cancer. All of it. I get checkups now and then, but that's all. You don't need to worry about that."

Mama said it like Isabel was a baby and didn't know anything. But cancer wasn't something you could count on to leave you alone. "I can worry if I need to!" Isabel said. "I'm a big girl!" Mama was always saying that she was a big girl, but if Isabel was so big, why didn't Mama talk to her like she was?

The baby's face collapsed into a frown, and it let out a whine. Mama lifted her hand from Isabel's head to jiggle the baby, and Isabel walked slowly up the steps to the house.

"Come back, honey," Mama said, but Isabel kept going.

In her room, Isabel picked up the fire-escape map the teacher had given back. Mrs. Shemeleski had given her a check mark, but it was no good. It was stupid. She tore it in half.

From under her bed she pulled out her markers and a paper grocery bag. Cutting the back open, she laid it out flat and began drawing a new map. There was her house, and there was Tara's next door, where lots of kids were playing in the yard. Tara's had a big X over it because it was off limits. Isabel's house had a huge baby taking up the whole bedroom. Mama stood at the back door, making sure Isabel was stuck inside. Sickness drifted like smoke around them, waiting and watching for Isabel to let her guard down.

Candy

Tara wouldn't sit with her on the morning bus anymore. She walked right past Isabel, giggling with the older girls and not even looking her way. It was Mama's fault, not hers, Isabel wanted to say, but Tara didn't give her the chance.

The boy with the squished ears sat next to Isabel, and she scooted as far away from him as she could, pressing herself into the bus window.

After the field trip, everything was back to normal in the classroom, and there would be no sitting with the pink and purple girls or talking about how she was funny. Courtney and Alicia didn't look her way.

Mrs. Shemeleski called Isabel to the front during silent reading time. "Is something wrong?" she said.

"Why?"

"You're all fidgety, and you look upset."

She did? Well, she *was* upset. Tara wouldn't talk to her,

and Mama might get sick again. No one was supposed to bother her here at school. "I'm fine," Isabel said.

"All right then," Mrs. Shemeleski said. "If you say so."

At recess Mrs. S. made all the girls play kickball. At least Isabel didn't have to stand next to a tree by herself watching for Tara. She tapped her toes as they lined up.

"Kickball?" Mandy whined. "I'm wearing a dress."

These girls were such wimps about anything outside, not like Tara, who played football with the boys.

Mrs. S. didn't budge. Everybody had to play. She put Isabel on a team with Alicia and Courtney, and they would have to play with her. Maybe Alicia would think Isabel was funny again, and they would like her. Alicia played pitcher, and Isabel covered first base.

A giggle bubbled up inside when Mandy, on the other team, got hit with the ball. "Ha!" Isabel cried, bursting out laughing, covering her mouth. She hadn't meant to laugh, but Mandy looked so stupid falling down in her prissy dress. Sometimes it was impossible to be nice.

When her team was up, Isabel got a run! Courtney and Alicia cheered, and Isabel let out a whoop. Courtney gave her a high five like they were old buddies. Alicia didn't seem so snotty today. Maybe she could be friends with *them* now, Alicia and Courtney and even silly Mandy. Maybe she would buy them lavender pencils at the school bookstore.

When their team won, Isabel did a little dance on the cracked red clay of the ball field.

After school Isabel stood under the covered walkway with all the pink and purple girls whose moms picked them up in cars, too. Maybe Isabel wouldn't even miss riding the bus. Tara stood across the front schoolyard, waiting with the other bus kids. Isabel was a pick-up kid now.

The pink and purple girls had all gathered around Courtney. Isabel peeked over Mandy's shoulder to see what was going on. Courtney had a folding paper fortune teller.

Courtney turned to Alicia. "You will marry Bradley and have fourteen green babies."

The other girls laughed, but not Alicia.

"That's not what it says! Let me hold that." Alicia grabbed the fortune teller. "Isabel," she said, turning to her. "Let's tell your fortune."

Everyone stopped laughing and looked at Isabel.

Was Alicia trying to trick her or was she letting her into the group?

Alicia's gray eyes glinted.

This was Isabel's chance to get in with her, with the whole group. She couldn't say no now. Isabel had four colors to choose from on the fortune teller. Purple. Then a number. Eleven. After that she had to pick a boy, and they were all bad.

"You will wear purple suits to your high-powered office job and divorce Jimmy after eleven years," Courtney pronounced.

"Ha! Divorced!" Alicia said.

She knew it! Alicia just wanted to make fun of her. "At least I don't have fourteen green babies with Bradley," Isabel said.

Everybody got quiet. Alicia narrowed her eyes at Isabel.

Mama drove up just then, and it was too late to make everything okay. Isabel was always saying the wrong thing. Hadn't Mrs. S. told her?

Isabel opened the car door, and everything from the day before came rushing back at her. Tara's house, Mama making a scene, her promise to pick Isabel up.

"Hey, honey. How was school?" Mama said, as if they did this every day.

Isabel got in and buckled her seat belt. Water from the baby's nose was dripping into its mouth. Why couldn't Isabel be in one of the other cars, one with a long-haired mother driving her off to a big house full of toys?

"I need some candy," she said.

"What for?" Mama pulled out of the school parking lot.

"A party at school." She'd give candy to Alicia and her group, and they would be her friends.

"I have some peppermints in the cupboard."

"Can we get chocolate?"

"Peppermints will have to do. I'm not making another trip to the store today. Remember tomorrow is support group."

Again? Hadn't they just had the sick ladies over?

At home in her room Isabel sat on the floor, drawing the sick ladies on the house map. They covered it like mosquito bites.

The pink and purple girls let her join double Dutch the next day, and Alicia seemed to have forgotten about the fortune-teller incident.

Isabel gave one peppermint to each girl. She was going to make them like her. They *would* like her. "That's a nice shirt you have on, Courtney." It was lime green with pink piping. There. That was nice. Even Mrs. Shemeleski would agree.

"Thanks," Courtney said, looking Isabel up and down.

Isabel's shoes didn't have the right blue rectangle on the heel, and she'd worn this pink shirt only last Friday. The girls let her play, but she could see they didn't like her clothes and would kick her out of their group by tomorrow.

The fourth graders were coming out now. Tara was surrounded by a bunch of laughing girls. She didn't even miss Isabel.

But at the end of lunch something good happened: the teacher said Isabel was a table-washer with Courtney! She almost never got to wash the class lunch table, and if she did, it was with the squished-ears boy. Washing the table was a special privilege, mainly because it meant you got to talk with your buddy and miss the first part of social studies. No one cared how long it took you to wash that table.

Isabel and Courtney grabbed the dishrags out of the bucket of cleaning solution.

"Let's go slow," Courtney said.

She wanted to be late to class with Isabel! Maybe, maybe, maybe she would invite her over this afternoon, and Isabel could skip the sick ladies.

They wiped the long plastic table in big, slow swirls, going over both sections twice and even waiting to make sure it dried. When they walked back to class, they took their time, stopping to get a nice long drink at the water fountain.

"Do you have any more peppermints?" Courtney asked when she'd finished taking a drink.

Isabel's hands broke out in a sweat. She had given out

all the peppermints. "I'll bring some tomorrow," she said, stepping up to the fountain.

"That's okay," Courtney said. "Hey, Isabel. Want to come to my birthday party?"

Wow. Isabel stopped drinking. "Yeah! When is it?"

"I'll pass you an invitation in class," she said, putting her hands in her pockets.

A party! After Courtney slid the yellow envelope across the floor to her, Isabel didn't hear anything Mrs. S. said for the rest of the day. Even social studies couldn't ruin her mood.

Mama didn't care what kind of shoes Isabel had to wear.

"Your shoes are perfectly good," Mama said on the way home.

The baby wiggled its feet, kicking off its socks.

"You don't want me to have any friends." Isabel kicked at the floor of the car.

"What do shoes have to do with friends?"

"Everything!"

Mama thought making friends was easy, that you could just decide you were somebody's friend and that was it. Or you could replace your best friend, no problem.

Isabel locked and unlocked the doors with the power button. "Courtney invited me to her birthday party."

"Who's Courtney? A new friend?"

"She's not a friend yet. She might be my friend, but I need new shoes."

Mama turned the car onto their street. "Do you remember Benjamin? He's coming to the meeting again today."

The sick ladies! She'd forgotten about the meeting after Courtney invited her to the party, and it was too late to make other plans now.

"I expect you to be on your best behavior," Mama said. "Be nice to him—do you hear me, Isabel? Or you will be punished."

The baby raised its hands up and shook its fists, like it was agreeing with Mama.

Isabel didn't answer. What could be worse punishment than having to play with the boy in the first place and having a bunch of sick ladies over?

She would pretend they weren't even there. No passing out iced tea or cookies this time. If she wasn't big enough to hear everything they talked about, she wasn't big enough to help.

"Isabel," Mama said, "remember how Janey was nice to you?"

When Mama had first made Isabel come to the meetings, Isabel was scared of all those ladies, but Janey sat with her and then took her to the park. But Janey had wanted to, right? Her mother didn't force her to be nice to Isabel.

"Janey doesn't come anymore," Isabel said.

"Yes, honey, I know. But Benjamin will be there, and he needs you to be his friend. Remember how scared you were at first?"

"I wasn't scared." Not like Benjamin.

The baby turned to her and bobbed its head, smiling like it was trying to make friends with her. She did not want to be its friend.

When the ladies began to show up, Isabel sneaked out to the back yard and behind the oak tree. She climbed up the first branch, but Mama saw her before she could get any farther.

"You know you're not allowed to climb that tree." She put her hands on her hips. "What's the matter with you, Isabel? I thought we talked about this meeting."

Isabel swung from the bottom branch.

"Your daddy's going to give you a talking-to when he gets home, if you don't come down right now."

It wasn't fair. Isabel didn't get to choose *anything*, not even what she did in her own house. She jumped to the ground, crunching acorns under her heels. Her blood was hopping. Mama could make her come inside, but she couldn't make her be friends with that boy. If she had to go to the meeting, she was going to stay for the whole thing. If she was such a big girl, she could hear everything.

In the meeting the baby sat on Mama's lap, a tuft of hair down the middle of its head—the same look Stirrup Pants had. The miracle baby got to hear everything. It didn't know what it was like to have a sick mother. It didn't know how to help Daddy with the laundry and never had to eat ravioli out of a can. It didn't have to play by itself because Mama was resting.

Mama told Isabel to pass out the tea, but instead she left it sitting on the kitchen counter. These ladies could get their own tea if they needed it so much. Isabel sat in the corner next to the end table stuffed with magazines.

Sure enough, the Ben boy came with his mother again, the hair at his crown stuck up in a clump. His mother wore a crinkly skirt with sandals and a paisley scarf wrapped around her head. Ben sneered at Isabel, and she glared back.

"Where's Barbara? Does anyone know how she's doing?" Big Hair asked.

"I think she's bad," Stirrup Pants said. "I think she's real sick."

See, Mama? Isabel wanted to say. *They do get sick again.* She shivered. *You don't need to worry.* Ha!

Stirrup Pants swallowed again and again, making

faces as if it hurt when she did it. Tears sneaked out of the corners of her eyes. She didn't boo-hoo, just let the tears slip out one by one and wiped them with the back of her hand. A grown lady crying in public like a baby.

The ladies' wrinkled necks and the feet smell of their pantyhose made Isabel want to shrivel into the floor. She closed her eyes.

Big Hair's voice broke through the ladies' chatter. She wanted them to close their eyes and imagine they were drifting away from earth. *No problem,* Isabel thought.

"Leave behind your worries, your lists, the things you haven't done. Leave them on earth and float up ... up ...," Big Hair said.

Isabel pushed the sick ladies to the back of her mind and thought about the party invitation Courtney had passed her. It had yellow flowers on it and a scalloped edge. She pretended she was at Courtney's house, eating an enormous bowl of Rocky Road on a leather barstool in a huge white kitchen. They would swing around and around on the stools and toss a ball for a curly-haired little dog to fetch. Courtney's mother would make them brownies and give them new notebooks with cat stickers.

Then they would go to Courtney's playroom over-flowing with Barbies and My Little Ponies, a big-screen TV, and a computer for each of them.

"... Float up through the sky and into space ..."

She would go to the birthday party in a new flowered dress and be Courtney's new best friend. Maybe Isabel would even have her own party when her birthday came.

She opened her eyes. Ben was staring at one spot across the room, not even blinking. Mama had her eyes closed, but the baby didn't. Stirrup Pants was making faces at the baby, trying to make it laugh.

"Good," Big Hair was saying. "Now let's come back to earth, but keep that feeling of peacefulness. Slowly, slowly come down," she said. "Imagine being in your own house, with a window overlooking anything you want."

Isabel closed her eyes again and scratched her ankle under her sock. She would want a window over the garden Daddy used to keep at their old house. It had butter beans and tomatoes, squash and bell peppers. Daddy and Isabel had walked barefoot in the soft gray dirt, picking vegetables in the summer heat. Isabel had gone out every day, looking for red tomatoes and swelling peppers. Since they had moved, they hadn't had a garden. Daddy didn't have time for it.

After the question of the day Mama tried to make her leave with the boy, but she wasn't falling for that trick again. If Mama talked, Isabel was going to hear every word.

Mama kept giving her looks, but Isabel stayed put. Finally Mama knelt down on the floor. "Isabel, it's time for you and Ben to go play," she said.

When Isabel still didn't move, Mama took her by the hand and practically dragged her into the kitchen.

"Why does the baby get to stay?" Isabel said.

Mama sighed. "Because she's not big enough to play by herself."

Of course. Only big girls had to do things by themselves.

Isabel snatched her hand out of Mama's and sat on the linoleum by the door. Mama slid the pocket door closed. The door slid open again, and in came Benjamin, his mouth pulled into a tight line.

"You can go outside," Isabel said. "I'm staying here." She pulled out her crayons and coloring books.

The boy just stood there like a lump.

Isabel huffed. "I guess you can color one, but you better not mess it up. Here, have this one." She held up the Porky Pig coloring book, which she never used.

He scoffed at it like the last thing he wanted to do was color pictures with her. Well, she didn't want to color pictures with him, either. Why couldn't he just go outside?

She colored the hem of Cinderella's dress a deep, even purple. Cinderella's hair would be dark like hers, and the dress pink and purple, with hot pink bows.

A lady was talking about her kids getting into college. Another felt bad for missing work because she was sick. One lady complained about her mother-in-law. Shrimp Boy looked up. Was it his mother talking?

"She's always coming over," the same lady continued. "It's really driving me nuts. It's awful, isn't it? I know she's just trying to help."

Ben sat down and picked up a brown crayon. He started coloring over Porky Pig's face with it.

"You're doing it wrong," Isabel said.

He looked up, his eyes flashing. He kept coloring over Porky's face.

Isabel narrowed her eyes at him. Fine. Let him think she cared.

Mama wasn't saying anything. Did she know Isabel was right behind the door?

She colored in Cinderella's magic pumpkin orange, of course, right down to the plush seats inside it. The pumpkin carried Cinderella away from her evil step-mother, away from the ugly stepsisters, to the fancy ball in her pink gown to meet the prince.

Some lady close to the door was saying, "Nothing tastes good anymore. It all makes me sick. Even things I used to love."

Benjamin looked up, then began coloring big black

marks over Porky's face. "We have to eat peanut butter and jelly every night," he said, grimacing.

Was he talking to her? Isabel looked him over. His mom must've quit cooking the way Mama had when she was sick.

"We used to eat ravioli from a can every night," Isabel said, sitting up.

Benjamin looked her in the face. His eyes had softened the tiniest bit.

"When Mama was sick," Isabel said. She shuddered, trying to block out the sight of Mama's gray face.

"I know," he said. He turned the page in the Porky Pig book and started over, this time with green, but he stayed inside the lines.

Isabel drew a trail of smoke out the back of Cinderella's pumpkin as if it were a rocket. Behind the door, Mama's voice piped up. Isabel put down her crayon. "When I was sick," Mama said, "all I wanted to eat was junk food. It was like when I was pregnant. Everything had to be salty."

Mama never talked to Isabel about what it was like to be sick or what being pregnant felt like. If she was such a big girl, why did the ladies hear more about it than she did?

"Is that your mom?" the boy asked.

"Shhhhh ..." Isabel strained to hear, but Mama had finished talking. Mrs. Andos was going on about some spaghetti recipe.

"She's not sick anymore? Your mom?" Ben asked.

Isabel closed her coloring book. Now *her* stomach felt queasy, and she couldn't color anymore. "I guess not," she said. Suddenly she didn't care what they said next door. She wanted to be anywhere but here.

Outside a truck door slammed, and the back door opened. Daddy! Isabel jumped up. He swung her in the air, and she threw her arms around his neck.

"You're home early," she said.

"We finished before we thought we would," he said. "How's my pretty girl?"

"Good!" she said. Daddy was here, and now she was fine. She smoothed the hair behind his ear.

"And who have we here?" He swung her around to his hip and faced Benjamin.

"This is Ben," Isabel said. "Mama's having a meeting."

"I see," Daddy said. "Hey, it's a nice day out. Why don't we walk to the park?"

"Yes!" Isabel said, leaning back from Daddy and jumping down.

Benjamin clutched the coloring book.

"It's all right," Daddy said. "I'm Isabel's father. Go check with your mom."

Ben hesitated.

"It's all right," Daddy said. "We'll be back on time."

The sick feeling rose in Isabel's stomach again. The boy had to come too? But she didn't dare say anything or Daddy would scold her.

Slowly Ben put down the coloring book and knocked on the pocket door.

To get to the park they had to cross the big busy street and go into the pink and purple girls' neighborhood near the school. Isabel held Daddy's hand and looked up at a tall brick house by the park. Was it Courtney's? Would she look out and see her with Ben? A little gray dog rushed out from the house, barking like crazy and snapping its jaws. Isabel jumped. She looked to the front windows. Had someone sent the dog to keep them away? But nobody was there.

Luckily they had the park to themselves. No sign of Alicia or Courtney. Daddy gave her a push in the swing to get her started, and Isabel swung harder and higher.

"Look, Daddy!" she said. If he would put up the swing set, they could do this all the time.

"I see you," he said, smiling.

The baby didn't get to go to the park with Daddy. It was too little.

Ben was busy kicking a tree trunk.

Daddy caught Isabel's swing from the front and let it go again, slowing it. "Why don't you ask your friend if he wants to swing?"

"He's not my friend." Mama must've been talking to Daddy about Shrimp Boy.

Daddy yanked her swing to a stop. "Isabel," he said, scolding. "The Isabel I know is a nicer person than that."

Isabel scowled. Daddy could cut her right through. "I am *too* a nice person," she said. But Shrimp Boy wasn't her friend. She barely knew him, and they didn't even like each other.

Daddy gave her a look that meant business, and she hopped out of the swing and walked over to Ben. "You want to swing?" she said, her jaw clenched.

He stopped kicking the tree. "Okay," he said.

Daddy pushed them both until they were flying. Isabel would fly away, out of here, down the street, across the state, back to their old house near the ocean. Daddy would get back his fix-it shop, and Mama would grow her hair long again.

"Wanna jump?" she yelled to Ben. He was probably chicken.

But Ben nodded. "Okay."

Maybe he was not as big a wimp as she'd thought. "Three, two, one!"

They landed on the sand, and now the playground was the beach, far away from the sick ladies. But soon Daddy made them leave, and the beach disappeared as they came closer and closer to the house.

When they got back, Daddy took the baby from Mama. "Hey, pretty girl," he said, and the baby smiled. He kissed the top of its head.

Isabel stared. *She* was his pretty girl. Anyway, the baby looked more like an old man than a girl, with its double chin and tuft of dark hair. It was only an it.

Ben's mother was ruffling his hair and looking at Isabel as if she was happy Ben had a new best friend. Isabel cringed.

Mrs. Andos was asking Ben's mother, "How's your energy?"

"It's all right, not great," she said. She turned again in Isabel's direction. "Oh, Isa—"

Isabel stepped back. "*Isabel,*" she said. Not just anybody could use her nickname.

Ben's mother smiled. "Isabel. Guess what? Benjamin is going to be transferred to your school, starting tomorrow." She laid her hand on his shoulder and smiled as if this was the greatest news in the world. "Maybe you can show him around."

Isabel's stomach tied itself into an instant knot. *No!* she wanted to say. She wouldn't show him around. School was the only place that Mama hadn't totally ruined.

"Maybe," Isabel said instead, not meaning it.

Ben was staring at his tennis shoes. He hadn't let on about anything. She wouldn't have gone to the park with him if she'd known. Now he was going to think she *would* be his new friend at school.

Mama stood there looking on, nodding as if her plan was coming together now. So that was it: take away Tara, tell Isabel to find new friends, and then run those off, too. Her friends had to be from the sick ladies' group, kids Mama picked herself.

"So Ben will see you tomorrow?" his mother was saying.

"Tomorrow," Isabel said, not promising anything.

Ben lifted his hand in the weakest of waves.

She couldn't wave back. It wasn't Ben's fault. It wasn't his fault he was weird and his mother was pushing him the same way Mama was pushing her. But she couldn't be his friend.

Ben and his mother walked out the door. Why couldn't he find a school of his own? Wasn't it enough that she had to babysit him here? If he followed her around, the pink and purple girls would never be her friends. Mama must've set this up.

Isabel went up to her. "You told them I would be his friend, didn't you? You told them I would show him around." She didn't keep her voice down even though there were still ladies there.

"Of course I did. Wouldn't you want someone to do that for you?"

Daddy turned to look at them, holding the baby on his shoulder.

Isabel huffed. "You made Tara hate me and now the other girls will too!"

Mama leaned against the kitchen counter. "If that's the way they act, they aren't really your friends."

Isabel stomped her foot on the floor. Did Mama think you could just go and get other friends, like replacing a bunch of broken crayons? "He's not my friend!"

The ladies got very quiet. Mama looked around as if she was getting embarrassed. "Go to your room, Isabel," she said, in a voice so calm and even that Isabel wanted to spit.

"You mean the baby's room!"

"Just go."

Daddy reached for her arm as she turned to go. "What's gotten into you, pretty girl?"

Isabel jerked her arm away. Mama had gotten into her, that's what. Mama and the sick ladies and now Daddy.

Had he known about Ben going to her school, too? At the park he kept calling Ben her friend. "I'm not your pretty girl. The baby is!"

In the bedroom she slammed the door and threw her stuffed animals one by one into the baby's crib. She pulled at Clyde the frog until his head was mostly torn away from his body. Gritty stuffing fell out of the gaping hole and onto the floor.

Clyde! She loved Clyde, and look what she'd done to him. She choked back tears as she rubbed his stuffing into the carpet.

Boyfriend

Ben turned out to be not only in her school but in her *class*. Right there by the teacher's desk. He was looking at her like he was drowning and she was the life preserver. Mrs. Shemeleski saw the look, and in front of all the pink and purple girls, she stopped Isabel as she was going to her desk.

"Isabel, do you know Benjamin?" she said.

Isabel's ears burned, and she tugged at her tights. This wasn't the sick ladies' meeting or the park with Daddy. Courtney was right there, with Alicia and Mandy.

"I think so," Isabel said. Alicia was grinning.

"He's new to our school today," Mrs. S. said.

Isabel knew that. "Hi," she said to Ben, as nice as she could muster. *Stop looking at me like that!* Didn't he know how to act?

"I think you two have something in common," Mrs. S. said.

What? The cancer? How did Mrs. Shemeleski know? Isabel pretended she didn't understand.

She sat down, put her books in her desk cubby, and pulled out her notebook for morning sentences. Why was it anybody's business if Mama had been sick? She wasn't supposed to be sick anymore.

"Benjamin, I'm going to have you sit behind Isabel."

No! she wanted to yell. "Courtney sits there," Isabel said.

"Courtney's going to move to the back," Mrs. Shemeleski said.

Isabel turned to Courtney. *Do something!* she pleaded silently. Courtney shrugged her shoulders and started packing her things. Now Courtney would forget all about her, maybe wouldn't even want her at the party.

Isabel turned back to the teacher. "Courtney needs to be close to the board so she can see."

"I don't know anything like that, Isabel," Mrs. Shemeleski said, and that was that. There was nothing Isabel could do.

Ben moved into Courtney's seat. Isabel felt like scooting her chair as far away from him as she could, but she stayed in her spot. Now she was going to fall to the very bottom of the class heap again.

Isabel was glad they weren't allowed to talk during

class. She didn't want to talk to anyone. She spelled everything wrong on her spelling test and couldn't get through
a word of reading.

If that's the way they act, they aren't really your friends.
But it wasn't that simple. She didn't have anyone else who
wanted to be her friend.

On the way to lunch Courtney was in front of her in
line. "Do you know him?" she whispered to Isabel.

"No!"

"I thought Mrs. Shemeleski said you did."

"No." She shook her head.

At lunch Ben sat beside her without even asking. *Be
nice,* she thought. *Wouldn't you want someone to do that for
you?* Mama had said. But it was so much easier at home
than here. Isabel concentrated on opening her cardboard
milk carton. She thought of Daddy. *The Isabel I know is a
nicer person than that.* So she stayed.

Ben blinked and blinked behind his big Harry Potter
glasses. His pink stick-out ears were the only part of him
that wasn't ghost-white.

Alicia and Courtney sat down nearby with their lunch-
boxes. Courtney pulled out her package of ham-and-
cheese crackers and small bag of peeled grapes. Why did
they have to sit so close?

"Are you going to eat that?" Alicia said, pointing to

Ben's tray of spaghetti. She was licking chocolate icing off her cupcake.

The other girls giggled. Isabel stared at her Tater Tots.

"Yeah, I'm going to eat it," Ben said, as if he didn't know what was wrong with it.

"Ewww!" Alicia said. "You know it's barfaroni. They make it out of monkey vomit, and it will make you barf if you eat it." Her eyes got big on the word "barf," and she grabbed her throat and pretended to gag.

Ben looked to Isabel for help. *She* wanted to throw up. Why couldn't Alicia shut up for once? But she couldn't say that or Alicia would turn Courtney against her. Isabel picked at her own barfaroni with her fork. Gross. The other girls had brought lunch from home—cheese slices and crackers, pita sandwiches, brownies, apple wedges, and juice boxes.

Ben was eating the barfaroni anyway, and the pink and purple girls had all stopped eating and were watching him.

"Yuck! I warned you not to eat it. Don't throw up on me!" Alicia scooted away even though she wasn't close to him to begin with.

Isabel couldn't eat the barfaroni now even if she wanted to. She sipped her milk. Were the Tater Tots okay? Surely not the green beans. What could she eat?

Isabel ate the Tater Tots and left all the other stuff. She kept her eyes on her tray for the rest of lunch. It was all she could do not to get up and move somewhere else. Maybe she should tell Mrs. S. she was sick and ask to go home.

But she remembered what it was like to be new at this school and how Alicia had made fun of her.

At recess, Mrs. S. asked Isabel to show Ben around the playground. Ben's eyes behind his glasses looked ready to drop big, fat tears. Isabel took a deep breath. Out the window the red leaves on the pear trees were starting to blow away. Other kids were running toward the playground, calling to each other, dribbling rubber balls and twirling Hula Hoops.

Isabel dragged her feet behind Ben and the teacher. Now was when she needed a magic pumpkin.

When they reached the playground Mrs. S. left them by the blacktop. They might as well be onstage in the gym with the whole school watching.

It was sunny out, but the soupy puddles of leaves hadn't dried up yet. A chilly wind sifted through the white oak trees. Boys were playing basketball on the blacktop. Ben should be playing with them like he was supposed to.

Girls didn't play with boys at school. Not unless they were going together, and they were *not* going together. Isabel didn't even like boys.

Alicia would turn on her, that the friendly act was just an act, but she wasn't going to let Alicia scare her off again. She had to put her in her place this time.

"Hey, Isabel," Alicia said, super-friendly, *too* friendly. Courtney and Mandy lined up behind her.

"Hey," Isabel said, playing along. Ben was still walking the balance beam.

"You're not supposed to be in this corner," Alicia said, all stuck up.

Isabel looked her straight in the eye. "So?" she said.

Isabel shot a look at Courtney, but she wouldn't even look at Isabel, just kept her eyes on Alicia. "We were just wondering," Alicia said, grinning. "Is that your boy-friend?" She looked back at Mandy, who giggled on cue.

Isabel got so worked up inside that she felt sparks flying out of her fingertips. Even the whole ocean couldn't cool her down. They didn't know what it was like to be the new kid. She hadn't had anyone to show her around, not even a shrimp boy.

Courtney's face was blank. Still she wouldn't look at Isabel.

Isabel got up in Alicia's face. "He's not my boyfriend," she said. Alicia could go swell up and bust, for all Isabel cared.

Alicia smirked. "Oh, yeah? Sure looks like it." She

turned to Courtney and Mandy. "Doesn't it, y'all? Barf Boy is her boyfriend."

Isabel was all out of nice. "He's not a barf boy, and he's not my boyfriend." She let loose, shoving Alicia backward and throwing her off balance. "*You* make *me* want to barf!"

Courtney and Mandy sucked in their breath. Alicia's mouth hung open, and her eyes got squinty and mean. She grabbed Isabel's shoulders, and Isabel pushed back, grabbing a handful of that blond hair. Ooh, it felt good to pull that pretty hair. Alicia screamed, lashing out with her claws, but Isabel grabbed her wrists so she couldn't scratch.

"Barf Boy!" Alicia yelled, still trying to grab at any piece of Isabel she could.

Mandy turned and started running. "Teacher!" she called. "Teacher!" Courtney was gone. Isabel didn't care if Mrs. Shemeleski came. She could watch if she wanted.

Then suddenly Ben came from behind and shoved Alicia to the ground.

Isabel backed up. Who would've thought he had it in him?

He was standing over Alicia, who had begun to cry. Miss Priss Pot was crying.

"You're in so much trouble, Barf Boy," Alicia said, whimpering. "You, too, Isabel! Barf lover! You're going to get it."

"Isabel, what happened?" Ben's mother asked her.

"It wasn't his fault. He was just sticking up for us." Us? Yes, she meant to say that. Somebody was on Isabel's side this time, and she wasn't going to let them blame him. *She* was the one who'd gotten him into trouble.

Alicia was staring at Linda's scarf as if it was the weirdest thing she'd ever seen. She'd probably go tell Courtney and Mandy how bald Ben's mom was. They would pick out anything different and make fun of it.

Where was Mama? Now they were all waiting for her. The house wasn't so far from the school. Why was it taking so long? Maybe she was at the doctor's office again. Isabel kept her eyes glued to the hallway, looking for Mama.

The principal came out of her door. "We're going to have to start without your mother, Isabel," she said.

Now Isabel thought *she* might cry, but she held the tears back. They were all standing up to go in when suddenly the hall door opened.

It was Mama! With Daddy and the baby, too. They had all come.

"What happened, Isabel?" Mama said. She had earrings on and her hair was fixed.

The baby kicked and smiled at Isabel, like she was showing off.

Alicia, Isabel, and Ben sat in chairs in front of the

Get what? What could be worse than being called Barf Boy's girlfriend in front of Courtney?

Alicia ran off, too.

Ben was standing there looking dazed, as if he wasn't sure what had happened.

Isabel sat down on the balance beam, the heat draining out of her and a deep heaviness rushing in. She felt too heavy to move from this spot, ever.

When Mrs. S. arrived, looking put out, Alicia was behind her, whining. "They attacked me, Mrs. Shemeleski." Her wad of yellow hair was matted with dirt and bits of brown leaves.

Mrs. Shemeleski shook her head. "Come on now," she said, motioning for them to follow. "All three of you."

Isabel slowly pulled herself to a stand.

"What? What did I do?" Alicia said.

Mrs. S. ignored her. "I thought you were going to look out for Ben," she said to Isabel quietly.

"I *was* looking out for him," Isabel said, glaring at her. Why didn't grownups understand these things?

The teacher marched them across the playground in front of all the other kids, who were lined up, staring. It was almost worth getting in trouble just to see Alicia have to walk like this past everyone.

The fourth graders had come out already, and Tara

stood in the back. She was looking straight at Isabel with a look that said, *What happened?*

Isabel almost smiled. Maybe the look meant Tara was still her friend.

Mrs. Shemeleski walked them down the main hall to the principal's office. Isabel had never been there before. What would the principal do?

On the way there, Alicia curled her lip at Isabel. "She started it, Mrs. Shemeleski."

What had ever made Isabel think she could be her friend?

Mrs. S. didn't respond. Isabel stuck her tongue out at Alicia, and Alicia narrowed her eyes. "Barf girl," she mouthed.

Isabel's blood boiled again, but she took a deep breath and kept quiet.

When they got to the office, Mrs. S. left the three of them on a bench outside to wait for the principal. Isabel sat on one side of Ben, Alicia on the other, while the secretary called their parents. She hadn't known about that part. Mama and Daddy wouldn't like this. Would they understand that she was just sticking up for herself? And Ben? Ben, who had looked so angry and tough when he knocked Alicia down, had shrunken back to a shrimp. He looked like the last kid who would ever get in a fight.

Alicia flared her piggy nostrils at Isabel behind B back. "You're in sooooo much trouble."

Isabel met her nose to nose. "So are you. She just ca your mom." She nodded toward the strawberry-haired retary.

Alicia pulled back and straightened up. She look around and started sniffling, as if she wanted everyone see how pitiful she was.

"You are so fake," Isabel said.

Alicia's mother showed up first, of course, with h pearls and perfume. She hugged Alicia hard and looked Isabel and Ben like they were ax murderers. "Oh, honey, she said. "Are you okay?" She put her arm around Alicia.

Alicia sniffled and shook her head. "They were so mean," she said, bursting into fresh tears.

Ben turned to Isabel. "What will the principal do?" he said.

"Don't listen to her," Isabel said. "Just tell the truth." Alicia assumed her pretty clothes and hair would get her out of everything. *Not this time*, Isabel thought.

Benjamin's mom showed up next with her scarf around her head, her forehead creased. "Ben, what's going on?" she said, laying a hand on his shoulder. "It's your first day, for heaven's sake."

Ben didn't say anything, just looked at the ground.

principal's desk while their parents stood behind. Isabel had never seen the principal up close before. She had tall, frosted hair and freckles on her neck.

She looked over a pair of half glasses at them. "So I understand the three of you were in a fight," she said matter-of-factly.

"They hit me!" Alicia cried, pointing at Isabel and Ben.

Isabel wanted to turn and look at Mama and Daddy, but she didn't dare look away from the principal. What did they think? Would they believe her? Would they be on her side?

"We did not," Ben said. His face was red, and the shrimp look had disappeared again.

"You hit a girl, Benjamin?" his mother said.

He shot a dirty look at Alicia. "I didn't hit her. She's a liar! I don't care if she is a girl."

Everyone went quiet, even Alicia and her mother.

Isabel couldn't keep a grin from spreading across her face. They would all believe Ben, especially Mama and Daddy. Isabel turned to look at them. The baby squirmed in Mama's arms, and Mama's and Daddy's faces were blank. Isabel turned back to the principal with a straight face.

"Isabel," the principal said, "what happened?"

Isabel felt her mouth go dry as she looked Alicia over. "She called us mean names," she said.

"I did not," Alicia said, making a face.

The principal gave them a once-over. "I'm suspending the three of you for half a day and sending you home," the principal said.

"But—" Alicia said.

"The three of you will meet together in guidance on Monday."

The principal opened the door and showed them out. Mama and Daddy still had barely said anything, and she couldn't figure out the expression on their faces. Were they disappointed, embarrassed, mad? What were they going to do to her at home?

The baby was the only person smiling, cooing away at everyone.

Ben looked at Isabel with his scared little eyes. He looked sweaty and defeated, even though he had won the fight.

"Thanks," she said. No one had ever stuck up for her like that, not even a shrimp boy.

He gave a little nod.

"Come on, Ben," his mother said, pulling him along. "We'll see you at the next support meeting, Marsha, Isabel." She'd probably never want Isabel to play with Ben again.

Alicia and her mother didn't give them a second glance on their way to the parking lot.

Mama was staring straight ahead, watching the others get into their cars. No one said anything the whole way home.

Rebekah

When they got to the house, Mama told Isabel to sit down at the kitchen counter, and Daddy took the baby into the living room.

Mama shook her head. "Was this girl one of your new friends?" she asked.

"I thought she was," Isabel said. "I should've known better. She's made fun of me since first grade. She said Ben was my *boyfriend* because the teacher made me take him around the playground. She called him Barf Boy." Isabel put her hands on the counter. "You told Mrs. Shemeleski he was my friend, didn't you?"

Mama pressed her lips together.

Isabel leaned forward. "She knew about the cancer!"

Mama frowned. "The cancer isn't a secret, Isabel."

Isabel kicked the cabinet in front of her. "It *was* a secret." The pink and purple girls' mothers had never been sick, never would be sick.

Mama came around the counter and sat on the stool beside her. She took Isabel's hand. "I'm sorry she made fun of you, honey."

She hated being different, being picked on. She let Mama stroke her hair until Daddy brought in the baby, who was crying, and handed it to Mama. Again, the baby came first.

Isabel blew out a long, slow breath, went to her room, and closed the door. From underneath her bed she pulled out another paper bag for a new escape map. She felt like she'd left a burner on inside her ribcage.

Before she could even get the house drawn, the door opened, and Mama popped her head in.

"Isa, I need you to watch the baby."

She didn't look up. "My name is *Isabel*."

"Isabel, then. Rebekah spit up in my hair, and I need to take a shower. Daddy's resting. I'll just be a few minutes."

"Fine," Isabel whispered, even though it wasn't fine.

Mama put the baby down on its back and left. The baby stank of sour milk, its clothes still wet with spit-up.

"Cancer makes you throw up," Isabel said, leaning over it. "A baby inside will make you throw up, too."

The miracle baby looked up at her and blew a spit bubble. It didn't even know what she was talking about. Maybe there was something wrong with it because of Mama's cancer. Maybe it had cancer.

"When you get cancer, all your hair falls out," Isabel said, pushing the baby's dark hair back from its forehead.

The baby squealed, as if this was the most fun she'd ever had.

"When she was sick, Mama's hair came out in the sink and the couch and the bathtub," Isabel told the baby. "You never got to see her with long, pretty hair. She used to be the prettiest mom in the whole neighborhood before she got sick. Before she had you."

Isabel got angrier just thinking about it. Because of the baby they would never move back to the ocean now. Daddy had to keep this traveling job so Mama could stay home with the baby. He would never reopen his shop. He would never be home to put her to bed every night and tell her stories about Clyde. The baby took every last inch of Mama. Mama would never grow her hair long again and put on her long swishy skirts. Now that the baby was here, they were stuck for good.

"Everything okay?" Mama called out from the bathroom.

"Everything's fine," Isabel said, teeth clenched. Even when the baby was happy, Mama thought Isabel was doing something wrong.

If Mama didn't trust her to watch the baby, then she wouldn't. She picked up a red crayon and began drawing again, quickly sketching in the outlines of the house.

The baby picked up a polka-dotted rattle.

With the red crayon, Isabel drew a fire spilling out of her room, scribbling it bigger and bigger until it covered the crib and reached into the hall.

The baby gurgled. Isabel put her crayon down and smushed the baby's big cheeks together into a fish face. *Pretty girl!* she thought, letting go of the baby's cheeks. Mama said the baby looked like Isabel, but the baby was fat with a mound of fuzzy hair. Isabel was skinny with lots of long, dark, wavy hair.

"Lots of things start fires," she told the baby. "Leaving the iron or the stove on. A mirror in the sun. Cigarettes." Cigarettes could start cancer, too. The sick ladies said so.

She leaned over the baby, face to face. If there were a fire in the house, Isabel would spray the fire extinguisher and call 9-1-1. Mama and Daddy and Isabel would run across the street to get away. But what about Rebekah?

Isabel would have to be the big girl again and grab the baby out of the crib. She pulled the baby by its arms so it was sitting up. It would be a long way to carry the blob, but Isabel was the only one in their room who could walk. The baby squeezed Isabel's fingers.

Mama and Daddy would be out on the sidewalk, waiting for her to rescue Rebekah.

Isabel would rush out to the street, out of the flames,

but the baby was heavy, and maybe she couldn't carry the baby all that way. Isabel was tired.

She was tired of trying so hard to be nice to Ben and the pink and purple girls. She was tired of trying to keep the cancer away from their house, and most of all she was tired of being a big girl for Mama.

The baby didn't need Isabel. It could be the big girl and take care of itself. Isabel didn't have to be big anymore, and she wouldn't.

Isabel yanked her fingers away from Rebekah. In her mind she was saying, *No! I won't be your big girl. I quit!* It felt good to finally know what she wanted to say.

The baby flopped to the ground—*boom!*—and its head landed on the rattle.

The baby shut its eyes tight and opened its mouth as wide as it would go, not making a noise. Could it breathe?

Wait! She hadn't meant that! Isabel hadn't meant to let her fall so hard. She hadn't meant to make the baby hit her head.

"Breathe, Rebekah!" Isabel cradled her head in her hands. *Please, please, just breathe!*

The baby let out a blood-curdling screech, then gasped for more air, screaming again when she had breath to do it.

If Rebekah could scream, at least she could breathe. Isabel yelled, too. "I'm sorry!" She hugged the baby, who smelled like Johnson & Johnson's baby shampoo. She felt her fuzzy head. A big knot was growing in the back.

Rebekah was just a baby, and Isabel had let her get hurt. Isabel blinked back tears. It wasn't the baby's fault Isabel was tired.

The baby looked scared, scared of *her*. Of course she was scared of her. Her own sister had nearly knocked her head open. Rebekah kept screaming.

Mama rushed in with her bathrobe on and her hair dripping. "What's the matter?"

Isabel turned. "It's my fault," she said, sniffling.

Daddy walked in, sleepy-eyed. "Is she okay?"

The baby wriggled and reached for Mama, as if Isabel were torturing her.

"Here," Mama said, reaching for Rebekah, but Isabel held the baby tight. "Isa," Mama said, loosening her fingers and taking the baby.

The baby took some big breaths and quieted to a whimper.

"What happened?" Mama said.

"I made her fall and hit her head." It felt good to finally let the tears go.

Mama checked the baby's head. "Rebekah is okay, honey. She has a little bump, but she's okay." She handed the baby to Daddy. "Isa, look at me."

Isabel couldn't do it. Looking at Mama's hard eyes would only make her feel worse.

But when she sneaked a peek, Mama's eyes weren't hard.

"Look at me, honey," she said again. She laid a hand on Isabel's head. "What's gotten into you?" She sat down next to Isabel. "Are you angry at your sister?"

Tears welled up again. Isabel thought of Rebekah's mouth wide open like that, making no sound. She shook her head. "No." It didn't do any good to be mad at Rebekah.

"Are you that angry at me?" Mama said.

Isabel swallowed. She was *something* at Mama, not just angry—something so mixed up she couldn't say what it was. "You don't care about me anymore," she said.

"Is that what you think?"

Isabel picked up Clyde's body, still half full of stuffing. "You keep telling me who can be my friend, and you don't know how hard it is to make friends. You act like it's so easy. And I'm sick of being quiet for the baby and putting myself to bed and doing everything for myself so the baby can have you. I want to move back to our old house and I want you to grow your hair long. I want Daddy to come home at night and tell me stories about Clyde."

"Oh, honey," Mama said.

She wasn't finished yet. "Why don't you tell me what you tell the sick ladies?"

"What do you mean?" Mama curled her arm around Isabel's waist.

"What took you so long to get to school? Were you at the doctor? Are you sick again? I don't want you to get sick again!" Isabel sucked in a breath and held it.

Mama looked her in the face. "No, Isabel. I promise. I'm not sick."

Isabel pulled back. "You can't promise! It can come back! You say I'm a big girl, but you think I'm too little to know anything!"

Mama ran her thumb along Isabel's cheek. "I promise to tell you when I go to the doctor and what he says. If you want to hear what we say in support group, you can stay for the whole meeting. Okay?"

Isabel had to look away or she would start to cry. "Okay," she said.

"Isabel," Mama said. "Talk to me when you're worried, honey. I'm going to try to do a better job of listening."

Isabel let Mama wrap her up in her scratchy bathrobe. She smelled like shampoo and baby's milk.

"I love you, every minute of every day, and I always will." Mama kissed her on the head. "So does your daddy. Little babies need a lot of attention, but that will change. It's already changing. Rebekah will become more independent. She'll want to be a big girl like her sister."

"I don't want to be a big girl anymore. And *I* need lots of attention. Not just Rebekah."

"I've been asking too much of you," Mama said, smoothing Isabel's hair behind her ear. "You're my baby, too. You always will be."

And that made Isabel cry even more.

"What happened to Clyde?" Mama said, picking him up.

Isabel took Clyde. Oh, Clyde. He looked so sad and broken. You would think nobody cared about him from the way she'd treated him. "I hurt him, too," she said. "Can you sew him up?"

"Sure. Sure I can, honey."

Isabel took Clyde and cradled him to her. He was going to be all right.

Guidance

In the morning Isabel peered into the crib to make sure
Rebekah was okay. Her head looked fine. She was still
asleep, her little mouth puckered up.

The escape map was still on the floor. Isabel crumpled
it and stuffed it in the trash. She didn't need it anymore.
Making escape plans wouldn't keep the cancer away any
more than it would change where they lived. Now she
would talk to Mama instead.

Mama drove Isabel to school and left the baby with
Daddy. It was the first time she'd been out of the house
with just Mama in as long as she could remember. Isabel
rubbed her finger over the ribbed fabric of her seat belt.

"I do want you to have friends," Mama said. "Good
friends."

"Tara won't even talk to me anymore," Isabel said.

Mama was quiet for a minute. "Tell me about your new
friends at school," she said.

Isabel stared at the red traffic light. "They *were* my friends, before the fight," she said. "Courtney invited me to her party."

"That's great! Why didn't you tell me?"

Isabel fiddled with the door handle. "I don't know if she wants me to go anymore."

Mama looked over at her. "The birthday girl was in the fight?"

"Kind of," Isabel said, trying to conjure up the look on Courtney's face when they were on the playground.

"Maybe you can talk to her, honey."

"Maybe." She wasn't very good at making up with people, but she could try. She could give Courtney a chance.

"And, honey, you don't have to be Ben's best friend. Just be nice to him, okay?"

The thought of seeing Ben at school again made Isabel's stomach flip, but she did want to be nice to him. He had been nice to her.

Ben sat next to Isabel at lunch again, but Alicia was quiet and sat far away from them. Isabel had never had a buddy when she moved to this school. Maybe things would've been better if she had.

Isabel picked at her French fries and carrot sticks. She

couldn't catch Courtney's eye. Probably Courtney didn't want her at the party, and what would Isabel buy for a present anyway?

"They took away my computer for two weeks," Ben said.

"Who?"

"My parents." Ben was wolfing down his corn dog. "What did your parents do?"

Isabel tore a pale French fry into bits, squishing the mealy insides around. "I get punished a lot. But not this time."

Ben put his corn dog down. "Why not?"

She lumped the potato mush to the side with her fork. "I don't know," she said, which wasn't really true. It was hard to explain. She didn't get punished because Mama understood what had happened with Alicia. Isabel told her what was going on, and finally she listened.

After math Isabel and Ben and Alicia all had to go to guidance instead of recess. Isabel was kind of glad. At least she had something to do at recess that wasn't in front of the whole school.

The guidance counselor had a soft puff of salt-and-pepper hair. Her dark, birdlike eyes were ringed with purple makeup. She sat in an armchair while Isabel, Ben, and Alicia took up three cushions on a stiff couch.

What exactly was guidance for? Isabel had come once or twice while Mama was sick, but then she came alone and only drew pictures.

Alicia piped up. "I just want you to know I shouldn't be here, so you can send me back to recess. It's all a mistake. I didn't do anything."

Ben rolled his eyes at Isabel, and she hid a grin behind her hand.

"That's very interesting, Alicia. What about you, Ben?" Ms. Guidance said. "What can you tell me about what happened on the playground last week?"

Ben blinked, then looked at the ground. "I shoved her down because she called us names."

"She was being really mean," Isabel said.

"That is *not* true!" Alicia fidgeted with the hem of her skirt. "They're ganging up on me!"

Isabel and Ben, a gang. It made them sound dangerous. Isabel smiled.

No one said anything for a long time. Finally the guidance counselor spoke again. "Let's start over," she said. "Let's meet each other again. I want you each to tell three things the others may not know about you."

It sounded like something Big Hair would say at the sick ladies' group. Again, the room was silent.

What could Isabel tell? The kids at school didn't know

Ms. Pam turned to Tara, who tilted her head, looking up at her mother.

"You can go," Ms. Pam said with a shrug.

Tara smiled, and now Isabel could, too. Tara *did* want to be her friend. Isabel and Tara walked in front, Mama behind as they headed down the sidewalk. It was like old times, only different. Mama had never taken them to the park before. Today there would be no smoking or bad words for Mama to worry about.

"What happened on the playground the other day?" Tara asked under her breath.

"It's okay," Isabel said. "Mama knows the whole story." She told her about Ben and Alicia and Courtney. "I should've just told her to leave us alone and gone somewhere else."

That was what the guidance counselor said. Maybe Isabel could do that next time, but it sounded nearly impossible to be calm with someone who was calling you names.

Right now she did feel calm. Mama was okay, and she was on Isabel's side. They were going to the park with Tara, and Alicia didn't matter so much.

Mama pushed them both in the swings. They swung up and out, and this time they were flying into outer space together, all the way to the moon. Isabel would grab

that Mama had been sick, or why the baby was a miracle, or where Isabel used to live before they moved here.

"He's not my boyfriend," Isabel blurted out, looking at Alicia. "My mother used to have cancer, and that's how I know Ben, because his mother has it too." She felt bad because maybe Ben didn't want people to know, but there it was, out there. She glanced at him, but he didn't look mad.

Alicia looked down, as if she might even feel the tiniest bit bad but was too embarrassed to say anything. For once, she was quiet too.

"That's all," Isabel said. "I don't have three whole things." That was all she had to say today.

When guidance was over, Isabel and Alicia and Ben rejoined the class, and all the girls had a bathroom break. Courtney was over by the sink when Isabel walked in.

Here was her chance. She had to say something to Courtney, to try at least to make things better.

Isabel walked up and stood by the sink. "He's not my boyfriend," she said, looking straight at Courtney.

Courtney looked down at the faucet. "I know," she said, turning off the water. Then, very quietly, she said, "I would've shoved her too."

Isabel blinked. She would have? So why didn't she?

Alicia stepped out of a stall, and Courtney shrank away.

She's scared of Alicia, Isabel thought. Well, she herself had been too. She could forgive Courtney for that.

"You're coming on Saturday?" Courtney said under her breath.

She still wanted her to come? "Maybe," Isabel said. "I think so."

Maybe she would go to the party. Maybe it wouldn't matter if Alicia was there. Maybe there would be cake and ice cream and a pony ride or maybe they would paint their nails. Isabel didn't care what they did. She and Mama would find a new flowered dress and the best present ever.

Mama picked her up from school, without the baby. She had her hair fixed again and earrings on. Rebekah and Daddy were taking a nap when they got home, and Mama began fixing peanut butter crackers. She handed Isabel a cracker, and Isabel licked off some peanut butter before stuffing the whole thing in her mouth. Mama handed her another cracker.

The school bus came rolling by, and Isabel could see Tara getting out and heading to her house.

Isabel put her cracker down. "Can I ever play with Tara again?"

Mama sighed and screwed on the cap of the peanut butter jar.

She must be thinking of the smoke and the back talk. "What if she came over here?" Isabel said. "Where you could watch us?"

Mama put both hands on the counter. "Tell you what. Why don't you go ask Tara if she wants to go to the park? Daddy's with the baby. It'll be just us girls."

"Really? You can leave the baby?"

"Sure, honey. She's fine with Daddy."

Would Tara want to go? She had given her that look on the playground, like she might still be her friend.

"Hi, Pam," Mama said. "I'm sorry about the other day. I was just so worried."

"Must've been, to say those things to me," Ms. Pam said, tight-lipped and sharp.

"It wasn't your fault. I'm so sorry, Pam."

Ms. Pam nodded. "Thanks, Marsha," she said. Her eyes looked a little softer.

Tara's face was blank. Was Isabel wrong about that look on the playground?

Isabel had better go ahead and ask her. She looked up at Ms. Pam. "Can Tara come play at the park?" Her voice came out very quiet and high-pitched.

a moon rock for Rebekah and bring it back home, right down here.

Rebekah was too little to swing. She didn't even know yet what the moon was. There were lots of things Isabel would have to teach her.

"Let's get doughnuts!" Isabel said on the way home.

"It will spoil your supper," Mama said.

But she gave in, and they got a half-dozen of the powdered cinnamon kind, squished but still warm from the fryer.

After that Tara sat with Isabel on the morning bus again, in their old seat over the hump.

The Party

Isabel stepped out of Mama's car in front of Courtney's short brick house. The house looked shy, hiding behind big bushes, and down the walk someone had planted sunny yellow flowers. Isabel held a present all wrapped up and a card she had made herself. Mama walked with her to the front door, and Isabel rang the bell. Through the glass she could see that Alicia was already inside.

Would Courtney like the art set? Would it be as good as the other presents? Would Alicia make fun of her new flowered dress? At school, Alicia pretty much left her alone now. In guidance she was even kind of okay, but this wasn't guidance.

Isabel was glad Mama had put on lipstick and a skirt. She was just as pretty as all these girls' mothers. "You okay?" Mama said, kneeling down beside her.

She wasn't going to let Alicia scare her away anymore. She gave Mama a hug. "I'm okay," she said.

"You look great, honey," Mama said. "So grown up."

Isabel looked at her sideways. Was she going to say she was a big girl?

"But not too grown up," Mama said, smiling.

Isabel did look good. She loved the new dress and the way Mama had pulled her hair back with a ribbon. Isabel told Mama good-bye when Courtney and her mother opened the door.

Courtney had a big smile on her face, and her mother had kind brown eyes, not like Alicia's mother.

Alicia spotted Isabel right away and gave her a look that said, *How did you get invited?*

Isabel looked straight back at her, and Alicia wilted. Isabel could be Courtney's friend if she wanted to, and she did want to.

All the girls were wearing colored plastic charm necklaces. Alicia's had the most charms.

Isabel touched her bare neck, but Courtney took her by the hand and led her to a table filled with felt, pompoms, glue, and glitter.

"We're making purses," Courtney said.

Courtney's mother was helping them sew and glue the pieces together while Courtney's little sister wandered around, picking bits of fabric off the floor.

Isabel decided to make a round purse, with a big, fat

flower made of felt and pompoms. Alicia eyed it with a smirk, but the other girls, who had all made square striped purses, admired Isabel's.

Afterward they ate pizza and cake, and then it was time to open presents.

Courtney opened her card first. "You made it?" she asked. "You're a good drawer."

Isabel had cut a scalloped edge like the one on the invitations and had drawn a forest of yellow-leaved trees.

Courtney liked the art set. "My mother's an artist!" she said proudly. "I can practice with her."

"What a beautiful card," Courtney's mother said. She had short, spiky hair that looked cool, and she had an easy smile. "You're an artist too, Isabel," she said.

An artist! Was she? Isabel liked the sound of it.

Grownups

Rebekah was learning to sit up, and her hair was growing in. Now she looked more like a "she" than an "it." Isabel could see something ticking behind those dark eyes. She would have to teach Rebekah how to talk, so they could know what she was thinking.

Mama was right. Rebekah wouldn't be a baby forever, and Isabel could even help feed her now, rice cereal and bananas that she mostly spit right back out.

She made Rebekah laugh by doing silly dances or balancing Clyde on her head. Mama had sewn Clyde back together and given him a new red bow tie to boot.

Mama bought Isabel new colored pencils and a pad of fresh white paper. Isabel drew pictures of Rebekah and Mama and Daddy. She drew her room, the living room, and the kitchen from the inside. Her favorite drawings were views of the house from the front and the back. In the back, she drew in the old oak tree and the azalea bushes and the swing set Daddy had finally put up when she asked. In the front she drew Daddy's truck in the driveway and the sidewalk up to the front stoop and herself sitting there on the steps. The sky was clear and blue, no more smoke. On the bottom of the second drawing, she had written: *This is where we live.* Mama put them each in a frame and hung them in the kitchen.

At the next sick ladies' meeting, Mama said Isabel could stay with the grownups for the whole time. Ben stayed, too.

Staying with the grownups was like mashing a blister until it popped. It was awful while you did it, but you had to do it to see what happened, and afterward, maybe you would feel better.

The only thing that really changed in the meeting was the ladies' voices. They got more serious.

"I'm tired all the time, so I know you're tired," Mama said to Stirrup Pants, who was talking about her last weeks of chemo. "The baby takes so much energy. She still doesn't sleep all that well."

Isabel didn't know that. She must not hear Rebekah in the night.

Ben's mom talked about moving into their new house. "It's good to have a project to take my mind off the treatments."

Ben stared straight ahead, not showing anything in his face.

A new lady with her hair parted down the middle said she couldn't bring herself to tell her friends she had cancer. She felt embarrassed somehow.

The way Isabel had? It was hard to understand that a grownup could feel the same way. Today the grownups didn't seem so different from her. They could have been Isabel and Ben and Alicia with the puff-haired guidance lady. They had the same questions Isabel did.

Afterward Isabel ran for the back yard like a rock flying from a slingshot. It felt good to be in the sunshine, out of that dark, serious room. Ben followed, and soon they were planning the next meeting. They would leave in the middle the way they used to and build a fort of pinecones and sticks.

Ben's mom stood talking to Mama until the sun was getting low.

Daddy was coming home tonight from a job in Rockingham. Rebekah would have to go to bed soon, but Mama said Isabel could stay up until he got home. They could have chicken casserole together, and then she would ask him to tell her a new story about Clyde.